Synthetic Sea

Franklyn S. Newton

Published by Hazeldine Books, 2024.

SYNTHETIC SEA

First edition. April 12, 2024.

ISBN: 979-8224827572

Written by Franklyn S. Newton.

For Dan, you're my best friend I couldn't have done this without you.

With thanks to Izzy and Nix for their wonderful notes and feedback.

Chapter One

The rain had slowed to a light drizzle, quietly pattering on the rooftops above. Ryoma LeBeau stood and listened to the white noise for just a moment more, reminding him as it did of the grey evenings listening to the frequent thunderstorms on his long gone home world. Opening his eyes, he made a move from the doorway he'd sheltered under, aware he'd been lingering in one spot for too long. It was a good vantage point for seeing inside the bar he'd been observing, but anyone with a lookout would surely have noticed that too.

A fine, greasy mist clung to every surface, making the neon lit street look smeared, impressionistic, and the roughly terraformed air feel grubby. It left Ryoma with the impulse to wash his hands just one more time.

The bar in front of him was The Satellite according to the sign above the door, tucked away from the packed main concourse of Scylla. Looking inside, it seemed to be frequented more by the locals - if you could call them that - than tourists. From what he had gathered, the workers here were largely on contracts that cut them loose after a few seasons, no more than that. The constant churn of people stopped anyone getting comfortable enough to talk about unions, at least by Ryoma's reckoning.

It was much quieter in this part of the city, mainly worker housing and bars on the cheaper side, as well as the less legitimate gambling dens. It was more to Ryoma's liking back here, and perhaps his target thought he wouldn't be spotted.

The case seemed straightforward enough. Elise Rearden, a mining heiress as far as he could tell, suspected her partner Dayne was either wasting away her fortune or spending it on someone else's affection. Either way it set her up for a clean settlement. Dayne had been taking a lot of short notice 'work trips' to Scylla, which was less of a colony, and more of a cluster of clubs and casinos situated between the two major systems. According to his citizens' profile, he was a researcher for a synthetics firm, nothing Ryoma recognised, but his workplace had him closely monitored. A couple of corporate security types followed him everywhere, but they wouldn't say a word to her about his activities. Not uncommon for people working in research and development, but it made her suspicious nonetheless.

Ryoma had taken the case with barely a thought, things like this were a credit a dozen, just another for a pile. Suspicious spouses were the basis of private investigation, but over time the cases began to blur and it made him feel like a sleaze, hanging around outside cheap hourly hotels. But it was easy money for straight forward work, people were never as clever as they thought they were. Of course there was no guarantee he'd find anything, but he got paid either way. At least it got him out of his cluttered apartment on Polaris, moping and drinking, maybe it was just the trip he needed.

He'd spent the first couple of days getting to know the area, keeping himself busy in the bars and waiting for Dayne to surface from the glitzy hotel he'd been holed up in on the main strip. Ryoma wasn't even able to get a foot in the door, it seemed they were installed with a scanner that could clock whether you had a booking or the money to walk in. There was an override for exceptions it seemed, he spotted a handsome young thing being led in by a woman wearing more diamonds than anything else, after she'd had a quiet word with the door staff. The thought had briefly flitted to mind, but he felt a little too run down to play at being a honey pot these days. Besides, from what he could gather Mr. Rearden didn't seem to swing that way. Instead, Ryoma opted to stay in a motel near the spaceport, cheap and cheerful, although clean air cost extra if you wanted it pumped through instead of the stagnant crap that hung heavily in the atmosphere.

He crushed his cigarette butt underfoot, feeling restless. Holding his rain-slick jacket closed against the breeze, Ryoma crossed the road to enter the bar, the warm light inside pulling him in. He scanned the cosy interior; coated polymer walls modified to look like a deep-mahogany, non-existent this far from Terra. It was a busy night, the tables were mostly occupied by off-duty casino staff, workers between shifts, some alone, some paired off. Tucked at the back of the room, he saw his target sitting in a booth. Judging by his loose shirt and jacket, Rearden was trying to look casual and fit in with the usual clientele but the way he sat, stiff and bolt upright - like he didn't want the fabric to touch him - made him stand out. Ryoma smirked as he made his way through the bustling crowd around the front of the bar, not a master of subtlety, this one.

He looked around uncomfortably. Whether that was anxiety at getting caught or being around so many people outside of his usual circle, Ryoma could only guess. Perhaps it was a mixture of both.

He sat down at the bar, between an exhausted croupier who looked about ready to fall into their drink, and a sickly sweet couple getting drunk and handsy, careful to keep the target in his peripheral vision.

Might as well get a drink while I'm here.

To fit in, of course. There were plenty of others drinking alone, probably burnt out from making nice with wealthy customers who didn't tip. Making himself comfortable, he flexed his right arm, clenching his fist stiffly a few times. The golden light rippled on the silver surface, catching on the engraving that began at his wrist and disappeared up his sleeve. Weather like this made his synthetic arm seize up, an extra level of effort was needed just to keep it moving some days. A newer model would probably be far more reliable, but parting with it wasn't an option, not for him.

"Can I get you anything, sir?" A dulcet voice broke through, and Ryoma snapped to attention. The bartender approached with a practised silence, dressed far more formally than this dive deserved, shirt sleeves crisply rolled to the elbow and waistcoat accentuating a narrow waist that Ryoma's eye clung to for a beat too long. "What can I get you?"

"Whiskey, no ice," he croaked after a second, his voice slightly hoarse from under-use, he'd barely spoken more than a few words all day. His shaggy damp hair clung to his forehead, and in pushing it back he noticed a few greys creeping into the sun-bleached chestnut.

Time for work, old man.

Blinking three times in a sequence, he activated the contact lens in his right eye. Glancing back across the room, he blinked again, as naturally as he could, triggering the shutter a few times, and sending the images back to the server running from his motel room. It used to be that his sister would run the search, she'd had a better eye for it. He watched the bartender nimbly pour a few drinks for customers further up the bar, until the interface over his iris flickered silently to confirm the man's identity. *There you are.*

Dayne Rearden was sitting across from a woman in a powder blue suit, her hair coloured to match hung loose at her shoulders. She seemed to be reassuring him about something, hand reaching across the table, trying to seem friendly but there was a cold formality about her. He blinked again to run a search for her, and waited for the system to feed back.

Nothing at all, not even an ID. Odd.

With a muted clink, his drink was placed in front of him, a napkin folded underneath to catch the condensation. He'd spent most evenings on Scylla pretending to read something on his watch to escape interacting with people, but the barman's curious smile loosened his lips. "Busy night?"

"Yeah, a lot of people on their way through to the Inner System, a lot of prospectors heading back to Terra this time of year. They leave good tips though." He paused for a second to evaluate the new customer. "First time on Scylla? Don't think I've seen you around."

Ryoma nodded; it wasn't a complete lie, he'd spent a couple of days in a noisy windowless casino the previous year, but all he could remember was being not-so-politely asked to leave when his credits ran out. Besides, the naive tourist thing seemed to work in his favour when he was scouting. People liked to talk if you let them.

The bartender pushed the drink across the bar, their fingers touching briefly as Ryoma took it.

"What do you think of the city so far? Pretty right?"

"It's certainly something," he mulled it over. "Ain't quite to my taste, the locals seem friendly though."

He couldn't help himself.

The barman leaned across the bar toward Ryoma just a touch, voiced hushed. "Maybe you haven't seen the best this place can offer. Are you staying here long?"

"Just a few days on business, then back to Polaris. Maybe you can show me around." Ryoma grinned wolfishly, trying his luck, mainly out of habit.

The barman smiled back at the attention, caramel eyes lingering on Ryoma's. There was a single diamond on one of his ears; perfectly clear the only way lab-grown can be. "I know a few good spots, might be more to your taste."

"I'm sure you do. Get yourself a drink, huh?" Ryoma slid a few loose credits across the bar, he always kept a little physical money on hand, for staying off the radar, amongst other things. The bartender smiled sweetly; he was a distraction, but at least he was a pretty distraction. "Something sweet."

"Hey, can I get some fucking service here?" A voice barked, shattering the syrupy tension. The pair looked to the other end of the bar in unison, where a red-faced man was glaring at them both.

"Looks like he's had enough." The detective murmured without thinking, and noticed his new friend's lip twitch with a barely suppressed laugh. "Sorry to keep you, darling."

"Just a moment sir." The bartender straightened his waistcoat and nodded in thanks at Ryoma. His face shifted from a genuine to a perfectly artificial customer-service smile as he moved along to attend to the waiting public.

Ryoma gazed into his drink wondering how else to pass the time, when there was a loud, nervous laugh from across the room, abruptly reminding him why he was there in the first place.

Keep it in your pants, asshole. Back to work.

Back in the corner, Dayne was now holding the woman's hand, but in a crooked unnatural way. His contact lens flickered and adjusted focus to get a better look. Something was being exchanged between the two, the edges of a glossy plastic harddrive were being passed between them, the woman subtly palming it. His enhanced eye just barely caught the split second where what he thought was an organic hand, split cleanly open at the palm and the drive disappeared into a hidden compartment. Clever.

Maybe this business rather than pleasure after all, or both. Blackmail? Insider trading? Couldn't be particularly legal to be conducting it in a dive bar, on an independent colony. More than enough for Elise Rearden to get what she wanted, and more importantly, pay up. The expenses on this case had been hefty, Scylla was by no means cheap. The contact shuttered a few more times sending the images back to the server. On the next table he clocked a brick wall of a man, obviously sitting alone. Not so clever.

Reluctantly, Ryoma reasoned he should probably go back to his room and type up his case notes, at least before he spent the night out and was too hungover to do it in the morning. He finished his drink, hoping the weather was a little better outside.

"Leaving already?" The bartender's voice was tinged with disappointment as he paid up. "My shift finishes at one, if you'd like to see the sights."

"Maybe I'll see you later," he said, taking the hint. Feeling a little smug, he pulled on his jacket and sauntered out.

Taking the leisurely route back to the motel, he wandered with his own thoughts for a while. With a few hours to kill, he'd have time to file his report with the soon to be Ms. Rearden, and head back later on, maybe that bartender would show him a decent time. Some company for the night couldn't hurt.

Somewhere behind him there was a click of footsteps, not uncommon, but they were oddly quiet, purposeful. He took a breath and focussed as he continued to walk; judging by the number and pace they were walking there were at least three people behind him. He sped up slightly and they matched his pace. He walked even faster and so did they.

Shit.

He took a sharp turn and ducked around a corner. The old bar district was a labyrinth of narrow alleys that was always threatened with being torn down but never quite happened. The streets were just wide enough for two people to walk through shoulder to shoulder; either side was a mix of bars, gambling dens, and apartments for the workers, in various stages of open, closed, shut down, or derelict. It was set far back from the shining casinos and clubs the colony prided itself on. Trying not to look back, Ryoma turned a couple of corners, doubling back once or twice in the hope it would fool them or at least get them turned around. He'd hoped to duck into another bar but everything around this area seemed closed, in various stages of decay tourists weren't meant to be back here. Another tight corner and the street seemed to narrow even further. Almost all of the buildings were boarded up now, and he felt his stomach twist with the realisation he'd lost his bearings. This was unfamiliar territory.

Suddenly, the footsteps behind him seemed to dissipate, perhaps they were lost too. Turning back to retrace his steps Ryoma turned a corner, walking straight into a man much taller and broader than himself. He began to half mumble an apology when he recognised the man. It was the angry customer from the bar, who'd interrupted his flirtation with the barman - Did he ever catch his name? Aaron? Olive? He'd already forgotten.

The man must have been spotting for Rearden, and noticed Ryoma lurking, or clocked his contact lens. Either way he'd ruined his cover; he cursed himself for making such a clumsy mistake and turned to run but the man grabbed Ryoma's shoulder with a powerful grip that could only be synthetic. He tried to shake himself free, using his own synthetic hand, and sprinted back around the corner. The half-lit alley was occupied by two other people of similar size blocking the way, bringing him to a stand still. Both seemed to have exposed synthetics of varying degrees, arms, eye implants, likely the brainwork that went with it. That much visible metal was showing off, it was likely private security, probably corporate.

Outnumbered, he looked around for a way out. Most of the apartments around appeared empty, maybe he could pop the lock and hide out in one of them until they passed, but the window of escape was small and closing. He could make it, maybe, slither away and hide, but his pride started to get the better of him. Ryoma's body had softened with the years but he retained the conviction that he could still put up a reasonable fight, when pushed. And pushed he was.

The pair in front of him reached out to grab him but he leapt back just in time, landing a blow on the taller of the pair's face, breaking his nose, blood splattering on the cracked concrete.

So you're not full-bodies at least.

The rush of landing a successful blow, was abruptly cut off when a steel fist met his synthetic shoulder, jerking him violently backward. Something dislodged internally, and as he regained balance he felt a sinking terror that his arm was numb. Before he could react, he was pinned to the wall, and a sharp impact knocked the air out of him. He spat blood, the copper taste was a familiar one. Looking down the alley, it was almost completely dark, a handful of windows were lit but no people were in sight. He wondered if that bartender would be waiting for him, if anyone would look for him, he had no family left at this point and friends were scarce. A powerful hand grabbed his jaw and forced him to look up, examining Ryoma's eye.

"Where does the feed for this go?" The taller of the men asked, a face like granite. Ryoma didn't respond, just glared up at the hired goon, leading to another smack. He felt warmth spill down his face, blood stinging his eye, his vision blurred. "I said, where does this fucking go?"

Ryoma's chest was thumping with panic, but he looked up at the men defiantly with a bloody smirk. "Like I'd tell you, jackass."

It was foolhardy, he knew they'd only hurt him more, but he didn't feel like giving in so easily. Not to shitheads like this. The man growled in frustration, punching Ryoma in the gut again. He fell to his knees, head swimming, wondering if this was how he'd die, over nothing. He wondered if Serena would be disappointed. He tried to stand, he wasn't built like he'd once been, but he could still try.

A boot on his back firmly pushed him down onto the rough patchworked street, his strength leaving him even as he continued to fight. There was a sudden shout in the distance, echoing footsteps running towards them. The voices overlapped with urgency, but Ryoma couldn't make out anything, too distracted by the nausea that churned in his gut.

"Shit... just take it."

An impact cracked into his skull, sending everything dark.

Chapter Two

Slowly, Ryoma regained consciousness; his ears ringing and his body screaming at him in a multitude of ways. It seemed they'd left him alone for now. He'd gotten off lightly, he supposed. His lungs burned, his head spun, right arm fully unresponsive, but he was alive and that was a start. Slumped on the ground, he tried to work out which need was the strongest. He blinked to try and reactivate the contact, but nothing happened. His eye stung, felt gritty. He tried again, still nothing. It was gone. "Shit."

At the edge of his mind, he thought he heard a muffled click of footsteps approaching. Someone stood over him, casting him into further shadow. Maybe those men had come back to finish the job, but the next expected beating never came.

"Sir?" A voice broke through the white noise. If this guy was here to kill him, they were taking their time, toying with him. Slow and calm, like afternoon rain. "You need help? A hospital?"

"No, no hospital." He croaked, trying to sit up. A medical bay on a rock like this would wipe him out for the month, enough to cancel out anything he'd make from this case, and they'd likely push for a new arm.

"You sure? Your arm looks broken there." The stranger crouched in front of Ryoma, close, but not too close. They wore a strange old suit, all black with a shiny lapel, and a stark white shirt left open at the neck. "Don't worry, I won't hurt you."

"My apartment is nearby," they continued, "I can try to fix you up. Do you think you can make it?"

He looked up at them. It was against his better judgement, but he wasn't in a condition to refuse. There was something about their eyes, even in the near darkness, that made him want to trust them. Mutely he nodded, and he was lifted up effortlessly with a cold but gentle hand. Easily a head taller than him at full height, they had to be approaching seven feet tall, he wondered if they were modded or synthetic in some way. Not his business. They carefully guided him down the street carrying the bulk of his weight and all the while he couldn't take his eyes from their bright silver shoes, reflecting what little light there was around them.

"It's just down here." The stranger said quietly, nodding towards the street corner. "These buildings here."

He tried his best to keep pace with them, uncomfortably aware of a sharp, troublesome pain from his ribs he hoped was just bruising. "You had a rough night huh? You got lost on your way back from the city?" They asked, glancing down at him. "Don't worry."

Ryoma looked up as they came to a stop outside a ground floor box-apartment, window and door frame crusted with rough oxidation. He slumped against the cold steel of the wall, trying to keep his knees from buckling.

"Thanks uh, sir? Xir?" His head still spun as he tried to speak, trying to sift through his muddied brain for words.

They laughed softly. "People don't call me that too often, but I guess it's right. I'm a little of both, a little of neither. 'They' works fine."

"Sure."

They fiddled with the temperamental keycard until the door slid quietly open and led him inside, ducking their head as they entered.

"It's not much I'm afraid." They stepped out of their shoes as the lights flickered weakly to life and removed their jacket to reveal a bright white shirt, rolling the sleeves to elbow. "Please, sit. You should rest."

Ryoma sat heavily on a plastic two seat sofa that took up the bulk of the living space, the cushions were much more solid than he expected, but he wasn't in a position to complain. He was fighting to stay awake, a combination of his current predicament and the strange drawn out evenings of this planet, catching up with his body. The stranger stood over him anxiously, looking him over in the light. "Do you remember what happened to you? Did they take anything?"

They think I've been mugged.

"Stood on some toes, I think, saw something I shouldn't have." He looked up at them with a wry smile. "Don't think I lost too much, mostly pride..."

"Shit, well hopefully you're not too hurt. Could you take off your... and I'll see what I can do." They gestured toward his shirt, then disappeared into the next room before he could respond. The compact but tidy living space was little more than a box, the living and kitchen areas overlapping into each other, the bedroom presumably through the back. Along one of the pale grey walls were a few framed pictures, hung up at regular intervals, black and white at first glance. A little human touch. Ryoma was surprised they were allowed that level of decoration.

"Nice place you got here," Ryoma said, mainly to himself as he shrugged out of his jacket and carefully unbuttoned his shirt one handed. "Minimal."

He shifted uncomfortably trying to test the limit of his right arm, looking at the shadowy reflection of himself in the engraved surface. Nothing. Through the haze of concussion he felt a creeping panic that maybe his arm really was broken beyond repair. He felt sick with it, the idea of losing another part of her. With his other hand he felt around the edges of the arm, still fused neatly on to his darkly tanned skin just under the collarbone, wrapping around the back the shoulder blade. Still attached at least. His ribs on the other hand stung badly at the slightest touch, a dark purple bruise blooming all the way down his left side as a grim reminder of the evening.

A door clicked shut and Ryoma jolted, his heart pounding, blood running cold.

"Hey, easy sir. It's just me. You've had a hell of a night huh?" The stranger said gently, cradling a scrappy tool box with other assorted supplies balanced precariously on top. Ryoma sat back, feeling embarrassed, and let out a shaky breath, trying to calm himself through sheer will. He couldn't look vulnerable. The heap of medical and mechanical paraphernalia clattered. "I keep some stuff around, for emergencies. I should be able to patch you up, if that's alright with you?"

"Sure, go ahead." The oddly dressed stranger set the box down on the small coffee table in front of him, and he noticed a smear of his blood staining their collar, marring the crisp fabric, so white it could have been a very pale blue. "Do all the mechanics on Scylla dress like you?"

A smile tugged the corner of their mouth. "This isn't exactly my day job, but I know a little bit about putting people together." He didn't respond, he often found people would usually talk if they wanted to. "I play at the Reinhardt most nights, it's a jazz bar near the main strip. Or it aspires to be one I suppose. Do you know it?"

"Heard of it." The name sounded familiar. He'd probably walked past it a few times in the last few days, working his way through the bars whilst following Rearden around the city. Hadn't seen them though, he felt like would have remembered.

"Used to work behind the bar 'til management noticed I was halfway decent at the keys. Next thing I know they're telling me to get a nicer suit and it's all music I like anyway, and they don't mind me playing all these ancient Chet Bak...uh." They cut themself off, looking embarrassed. "Sorry, you're hurt, you don't want to hear me go on and on about nonsense."

"It's alright, I could do with the distraction." Their voice was a comfort against the quiet dark.

"I'm sure you could, the state you're in." They looked him up and down, eyes lingering for a little longer than they needed to.

"Wasn't my finest hour, that's for sure."

"So, you lose all your credits in a casino? Or maybe you won a little too much...they don't like that," their tone suggesting they knew from experience.

"Something like that." He was half tempted to continue, but he bit his tongue for now. For all he knew he wasn't entirely safe yet, giving away too much was unwise.

"May I start?" They took his lack of resistance as a sign, and got to work, glancing over him as they neatly rolled their sleeves up. Frowning, they touched his chin just barely to tilt his head back and examine his eyes. "Looks like you've had a contact lens in there too, did they take it?"

Ryoma nodded in the affirmative, and tried not to twitch as they took a closer look. He could barely stand touching his own eye, let alone other people.

"Looks like it was pulled out pretty roughly, but I can't see any damage to your eye, are you having trouble seeing?"

"You could say that, my head's not feeling so great." Ryoma looked up, trying to focus on the rivets in the ceiling and not the cool touch of their fingertips; like the first flakes of snow on his cheek.

"Any nausea?" They hummed, continuing their diagnosis.

He nodded. "Although a couple of kicks to the gut'll do the same, so who knows."

They smiled grimly at his bluntness and got to searching through the toolbox for what they needed. "It could just be shock, if you wear it often. It could take a day for your organic to adjust without it."

Abruptly, they disappeared behind him and knelt on the floor next to the sofa to match his level. He turned a little, to give them a better view and stifled a shiver as they began to detach the plating from his shoulder. The stranger hummed softly while working, dropping the minuscule screws on the coffee table in a neat row to keep track. It wasn't a tune he recognised, but it was pleasant; he wondered if it was one of the songs they played. Despite everything, he felt strangely relaxed in their hands.

Normally he hated this part. Even in his boxing days he could soak up punches easily enough, but it was the maintenance afterwards that made him squirm. Some mech-medic with too rough hands rooting around inside his shoulder, berating him for tensing up. But this was altogether different, calmer. They were experienced, that was for sure, it made him wonder if they moonlighted as an unlicensed mechanic in their spare time. They wouldn't be the first. The stranger made an awkward noise, like a cross between a hum and cough, to get his attention.

"Your arm's popped out of alignment. It seems you took quite a beating." They gripped his shoulder firmly in one hand and wrist in the other, the pinch causing Ryoma to wince. "It's fixable, but this part will sting quite a bit."

"What will?...Ow fuck!" He yelped as his shoulder clunked back into position, the suddenness and intensity of the pain making him taste bile. Ryoma took a breath to readjust before he realised he could feel his right arm again. "Shit, your bedside manner could do with some work."

"Sorry, it's better to do it quickly. Uh, here I'll get you something." They got up and opened a small fridge across the room. There was a rattle and a hiss, and he was offered a rapidly condensating bottle, by way of an apology. "I haven't got any painkillers, but it shouldn't get any worse. I'm afraid I'm not much of a nurse."

Could have fooled me with all that kit.

"Good enough for me." He took a swig. If they were going to poison him, he'd be glad for the rest. The liquid was so cold it barely had flavour, it might have been beer, but at least it washed away the lingering taste of copper. Pressing the cool glass to his aching head, he glanced around the tiny apartment cautiously whilst they continued tweaking inside his shoulder. A typical seasonal worker's place, just enough space to eat and pass out in between shifts, sometimes shared between a day and night shift worker. He'd seen a couple during his stay, although under far better circumstances.

"Anyone else live here?" Any more strangers or surprises that night would have to wait until he'd had a few hours sleep.

"It's just me here, I like my own space." He felt the surface plate of his shoulder reattach with a click, their whispered voice counting backward through each miniscule screw they'd named; a ritual just between them. They patted him on the back to indicate they were done and stood upright, rubbing curiously at the blood stain on their collar.

Ryoma looked at the toolkit they'd used, not dissimilar to the one used by his mechanic, but more dated, the case chipped on the corners and geometric shapes had been scribbled all over with marker. Perhaps they had some synthetics hidden under that suit, synth-skin was barely noticeable on some models nowadays.

"Your arm is an older model, the BioMech Helios right? I recognised the tempered steel coating."

He nodded. They had a good eye, especially considering how old it was. He expected nagging about it being outdated, the specific model had been out of production for nearly a decade, but that wasn't what followed.

"I thought so. It's a good one, you've kept it well maintained too. The outside is pretty tough, solid construction, not indestructible though. Especially if you're getting knocked around like this," they said, tapping his bicep and pulling up a chair opposite him. "Not that much different from organic, huh?"

"Yeah... always meant to get a newer one but I got attached to it, in a sense. Got it modified too and didn't feel right to let go 'less I really had to."

"Nothing wrong with that, if it works, it works." They reached out and held his forearm with such delicacy he barely felt them. "Could you test the movement for me?

Ryoma nodded silently, trying to ignore that little jolt that leapt up his arm when they had touched him. He flexed his wrist, making a fist a few times to test the responsiveness.

Much better.

The stranger gently pressed on the palm of his hand and wrist, and nodded confidently, quickly tucking their black hair behind their ears to keep from falling over their face. "No damage to the nerves by the looks of it, articulation good, neural connections are fine."

"Uh-huh." Usually he tuned out whenever a mechanic tried to explain anything to him, all he needed to know was if it worked.

They smiled at his bemusement. "It means you'll be ok."

"Ah, thank you." Ryoma winced, rubbing his temples as the beginnings of a migraine crept in. He'd been wearing his contact for the past few weeks solid as a memory assist and things felt strangely blank without it.

"There's no scratching to your cornea, though it'll feel bruised where they held your eye open to take it. You're lucky they stole it so cleanly, they must have been professionals. Anyone else and you'd need to pay out for a synthetic replacement."

"I guess so." He breathed a sigh of relief and took a celebratory drink; any eyework would put him out of commission for weeks whilst the nerves adjusted. Maybe it was a sign, he could barely stand touching his eye to put the thing in but without a second set of eyes on a situation he'd needed it. "Lucky lucky me."

They leaned back in their chair, uncomfortably far, into what could tentatively be called a kitchenette and fetched themselves a drink from the same fridge. A clear bottle of something he didn't recognise, emerald green and slightly viscous.

"Well, to luck." They raised their bottle slightly, tapping the neck against his drink in a lacklustre toast. He laughed drily and drank with them.

"So, you lose your licence for pilfering parts or something?" Ryoma asked curiously. "Never heard of a musician moonlighting as a mechanic."

"Like I said, I know my way around a synth or two, you pick these things up out here." Ryoma got the feeling they were underselling it, considering they knew exactly how to help, knew the exact model he had. They eyed their work as they took a slug. "Does it feel ok?"

"It's much better actually...thank you." He rolled his shoulder back to try it out. A little tight but some stretching and a long nap would probably handle the aching in his bones.

"Good," They smiled, chest swelling a little with pride. "It's a good arm. If you look after it, it'll last as long as you do."

"I'm hoping that'll be a while yet." He watched them take a sip. "Does my saviour have a name?"

They seemed surprised to be asked. "I'm Guin. Just Guin." *Short and sweet.*

"And you?"

"Ryoma LeBeau, just Ryo if you're a friend. And you seem pretty friendly." He couldn't help but flirt, even like this. He could have given a false name, he usually had one or two in the back of his mind when he was working, but he felt so at ease with them, he plain forgot.

"Well, *Ryo*, you should make a full recovery, but I'd get a specialist to check that shoulder joint won't decouple. Just in case." Something in his gut told him he wouldn't have to. "I wouldn't go getting into any more fights for a while at least."

"I don't plan on it," he shrugged. "But you know how it is."

"Can't say I do," Guin said, a smirk clung to their lips as their eyes scanned down, something had evidently caught their eye. "Don't want to scuff up that lovely engraving work."

"You like my dragon?"

He perked up and rotated his arm to let the engraving shimmer in the light - like the sea's surface in the midday suns. The creature wrapped around his arm from shoulder to wrist, a pair of tails trailing behind it. He liked showing it off, a gift from his sister, one of the few things left of her.

"Is that what it is? It's pretty, I've never seen one before." Their eyes glittered, enraptured by the image.

"A twin-tail? They're everywhere on Polaris, about this big." He held up his bottle, and then downed the rest of the contents, hoping it would at least muddle the pervasive ache in his side. "Someone brought a few with them to the planet about half a century ago and they did what animals do. Local government try to clear them out every couple of years," he rotated his arm again to let it catch the light for his own amusement. "But they keep on bouncing back, tough little buggers."

"That's a good animal to have on your side. Although, that said..." They nodded toward the dark bruising creeping on his side. "Might want to get that checked out, could be internal if you're that badly bruised up."

Ryoma could feel it, the impact on his body, the groaning ache of muscle pain. But nonetheless he shook his head, he didn't want to look weak.

"I've dealt with worse. Used to fight for a living, a long time ago." Although back then, he'd be in a better state, even after a bad loss. His spirit seemed to leave him abruptly, and he felt hollow. He talked too much, no one wanted to hear about an ageing failure's past exploits. Rolling his shoulders he reached for his shirt and threw it over his shoulders wincing at the tightness in his arm. The fabric was tacky to the touch with sweat and blood, but he felt self conscious about sitting half naked in a stranger's home, battered and bruised. "I've intruded on you enough, I should really get going. I'm sure the coast is clear by now."

"Wait," Guin said suddenly, standing to join him. "Let me... let me clean this up at least." They indicated the cut on his forehead, and dug through the first aid kit, their empty bottle abandoned on the coffee table.

Obediently, he sat back, a little more comfort couldn't hurt. They deftly unravelled and tore off a piece of gauze, popping open a package of saline to soak it in. The moment was oddly intimate as Guin stood over him and carefully wiped the wound clean, with so little pressure he barely felt it. As they worked he finally got a good look at them with his vision intact. They were a little paler than him, their hair almost blue black. They glanced down periodically as they worked, and he noticed the emerald green of their eyes, one slightly flecked with hazel around the iris. He felt an itch in his palms, the temptation to pull them onto his lap and taste that soft little smile. They'd look so pretty on top of him.

"Didn't think my night would end like this." He murmured without really thinking, glad he hadn't said anything more.

What am I doing?

"Me neither." Ryoma could swear he saw a slight blush on their cheeks in the warm half light of the apartment. They bit their soft pink lip, trying to stay focused on dressing the wound and not on Ryoma's own deep brown eyes watching them intently. They reached into their box of tricks once more, breaking the seal on a small can of hypo-bandage, the spray softly hissing as it was applied over the grazing on Ryoma's forehead. "Well, it looked worse than it was, your head might be pretty sore but that cut should seal up overnight. You might get a small scar, but it should be easy to laze if that bothers you."

Their gaze glanced over his chest for the briefest moment. He had other scars too.

"I think I'll keep it, it'll fade eventually. " He touched the wound curiously, his hand now coming away clean. His father had told him that scars were evidence he'd lived, choices and mistakes both, something worth keeping. He wondered if they had any of their own. "Suits me don't you think?"

"I suppose it does in a way. Have you got anyone that can pick you up?" They began to pack away their equipment, taking care to be quiet. Ryoma shrugged, Scylla wasn't his usual haunt, and his contacts were thin on the ground regardless of location. Most of them had been Serena's friends, and he'd pushed most of them away save for old training buddies of varying reliability. Guin shifted on their feet and looked through to the back room. "You can stay the night, if you need to."

"Are you sure? I could be anyone you know. I might be dangerous." He felt his old self confidence return to him.

"You don't seem very threatening to me." There was that smirk again. "I think I could handle you."

I bet you could.

Guin offered their hand, which he took gratefully, allowing them to take his weight with ease. Through the back was the bedroom; almost bare, aside from some basic furniture, it was like they never used it. "You new in town?

"No, I've been here for a while. Here, I have something that should fit you, I think." They slid the wardrobe open and took out a fresh shirt, giving him a glimpse of something glamorous inside, shimmering in the low light. They placed it down on the bedside table, and hovered in the doorway. It seemed like they didn't want to leave, their lips half forming words. Maybe they wanted to stay. Part of him wanted them to. Instead they flicked on the bedside lamp. "Try to sleep on your back, you don't want to put weight on it yet."

"I'm sure it's just fine, darling." The pet name slipped out before he could stop himself. Ryoma hurriedly thanked them again before they could react, and they left him to sleep with that tight smirk on their lips. He kicked off his miserably scuffed shoes and considered trying to stay awake, but instead he collapsed on the bed, too exhausted to be on guard anymore. Fidgeting on the stiff unyielding mattress, he eventually found the least painful position to lie in and listened to the light domestic clattering through the door for a few minutes. He wondered just who they were, the angel who'd quietly stitched him back together until finally he began to drift and slipped into an anxious, unsettled sleep.

Chapter Three

Ryoma woke with a start, panic gripping him briefly at his unfamiliar surroundings. The shadowy clutch of a nightmare slipped away, the details eluding him as he tried to remember. The wet splatter of blood on the street. Weak sobbing. Rubbing his face, he tried to piece together the previous night and shake off the dull ache encompassing most of his body. He reached out for the crisp satin shirt that had been left neatly folded for him, and slowly stood. Gingerly examining himself in the mirror, he assessed the damage. The hypo-bandage had done its work, sealing the cut above his eye and reducing it to a pale scar, but the deep purple-yellow stain on his ribs would need longer. He inhaled sharply through his teeth at the slightest touch. They were probably fractured.

You're too old for shit like this.

For the first time in a while he registered the almost invisible uniform scars along his chest, remembering the way Guin's eyes cast down to them so very briefly. Not in judgement or even curiosity, more like recognition. Serena had been so happy to have a brother, the two of them working to save for his procedures, she'd even helped him pick his name, Ryoma. It was their great-grandfather's she'd told him. He remembered his sister watching over him during recovery, and keeping him occupied with her endless talk about her plan to set up a detective agency in the Outer System; he hadn't been convinced at first, but she was so resolute, he was talked into it eventually.

A few years later, she was gone.

Ryoma huffed; all this over a few pictures of a man in a bar. Dressing very carefully; he tried the shirt. The cut and fit of it was vintage, easily older than him, but the fabric pristine and well kept. It was snug on his broad shoulders and slightly long for his height, but presentable enough when tucked in and the top buttons left open. He pushed his now slightly lank hair back, and paced the room a couple of times to get his bearings. It was almost embarrassing to face the stranger who'd gone to such trouble to help him, like bumping into a colleague who'd seen him make an ass of himself. Ryoma listened at the door for a minute and heard a soft cooing and baby talk, piquing his curiosity.

Cracking the door, he saw Guin crouched in the tiny kitchen area, being accosted by a malnourished orange cat that wailed and chirped at random intervals. They pushed a shallow dish of pale pink mush towards it, clucking their tongue, until the creature hungrily began to gulp it down. They caught sight of him in the doorway, looking him up and down, examining their handiwork.

"You made it through the night at least. I can't be that bad a nurse."

"Better service than most mechanics actually." The thought of them touching him slipped into his mind briefly, their lip between their teeth with concentration... He looked down to the cat licking the bowl clean. "Is that yours? I haven't seen any wildlife since I got here."

They shook their head. "Showed up a couple of weeks ago, I think she was left behind, poor thing. You get evicted from Scylla once your contract's up, and people can't always take everything with them."

The scrawny thing chirped at his presence, and trotted over for attention. He tentatively stroked her between the ears as she weaved between his legs leaving a fine coating of fur all over them. "I'd say she likes you."

"It's good she's got someone looking out for her." He smiled at the quiet domesticity, noticing the crumpled blanket on the sofa. They must have had no sleep at all, curled up awkwardly on that plasticky couch. "It's sweet of you."

"I do what I can." They looked up at him with those mismatched green eyes. "Speaking of neglected things, how are you feeling this morning?"

"Pretty sore, but still breathing. I think I owe you one." He chuckled drily and joined them on the floor. His hand brushed theirs as he eased himself down, and he thought he saw them crack a small smile at his touch.

"It's nothing, really. Just wanted to help." A handful of silver piercings climbed up the shell of their ear, shimmering as they shook their head. Ryoma wondered if they realised they'd left their hand where it was, just barely touching his. He wondered if he was thinking about it too much. They both sat in silence for a moment and watched as the now well-fed cat stretched and hopped out through the open window, presumably to look for more sympathetic locals and a second breakfast.

Ryoma racked his concussed brains trying to think of a way to repay them. A lot of things sprang to mind, but few seemed appropriate. That never stopped him before though, his bluntness made him few friends but made hooking up easy. Until now. Finally an idea struck him, he rifled through his pockets and produced a creased business card from his jacket. The last one. He handed it over after smoothing it out on his knee. "Here, if you ever need a favour you can find me here, darling."

LeBeau Investigations, All Cases Considered.
Sliding Rates Available.

The office address was crossed out and the contact number was scribbled on the back from when he'd updated it. Leaving it up to them seemed like the right thing, they'd come to him if they wanted to. He hoped they would. Guin cocked a carefully plucked eyebrow at the pet name and read over it curiously. "A detective, and Polaris based too? It's nice there."

"It is, well, part of it is." Usually words came a lot easier to him, he told himself it was the lack of coffee. "Have you been there before?"

"A long time ago. It's very different now, I imagine." They turned it over in their hand, running their fingers along the creases. "Things can change so fast it's hard to keep up sometimes."

"There's always something going on, especially in the Under city."

"And that's where you're from." Spoken somewhere between a question and a statement.

"Good guess, how'd you know?"

"You're too nice to be from the Upper, and that accent too. Deep Under City twang, with a rock hopper lilt, am I right?" Of course. "Maybe I'll give you a call."

"Anything at all, even just a social call," Ryoma said, his gaze lingering for a second too long.

Now you sound desperate.

He stood and straightened his jacket, trying to suppress a wince where his ribs ached. "I should get out of your way, you're probably wanting to get some sleep."

"Oh sure." They sounded slightly surprised, hopped up to open the door for him, and nodded towards the street corner. "You can pick up a taxi a few minutes from here, they won't pick up from the worker blocks."

"Thank you Guin, you really saved me." Part of him wanted to say something, anything else so he could stay a little longer.

"Perhaps I'll see you again, Ryo." His name sounded good on their lips.

"It's a smaller world than you think."

As the door shut behind him, Ryoma let out a breath that turned into laughter; he was much too old to feel like this about someone he just met. He headed off in the direction Guin had mentioned, following the increase in noise until he found the busy main street. The gloomy mid morning light was compensated by the lurid flicker of neon from the casinos and bars, making it seem like early evening already. His tolerance for noise and crowds was lower than ever, and this place seemed suffocating outside of the calm of the apartment he'd just left. The sense of quiet safety, gone.

Waving down a taxi, Ryoma slumped in the back seat, directing the ai driver to the motel. He'd need to leave for home soon, he thought, flexing his newly repaired hand. A cluttered little box barely bigger than the one he'd just left, but in his mind now seemed cavernously empty. Above him the thin atmosphere that clung to Scylla fell away into the sprawling vacuum.

Chapter Four

B ack at the motel, Ryoma made a beeline for the bathroom. He showered, turning the hot water up as high as he could tolerate in an attempt to soak away the stiffness where his arm was bolted in. The pain had lessened but it would linger for a few days. He longed for a bath, and an arm he could safely submerge.

As he shaved, he carefully inspected himself in the chipped mirror, the mottled purple of his ribs now far clearer. Perhaps he should take his nurse's advice and take it easy. His thoughts lingered on Guin for a second, the image of them leaning over him as they'd tended to his injuries seemed to stick in his mind's eye. He pulled their shirt back on, the scent of them returning him to that room. Ryoma caught himself and shook his head, trying to clear the thought of them from his mind, to focus on anything else. He still had to decide what to do with the previous nights' recording.

Close the case first. Then you can rethink your life.

He switched on the coffee machine, pouring the gritty dregs of the previous day into a shrivelled pot plant. Tugging on his last fresh set of clothes, and making a mental note to return the shirt he'd borrowed, Ryoma sat at the dressing table that had become his temporary office, heaped with drink cans and various forms of takeout he'd been living on. Nowhere on

Scylla seemed to sell the dumplings he liked. He listened for a moment as the coffee machine gurgled to life and gathered his thoughts. Chin resting on his silver hand, he reviewed his inbox with little enthusiasm. A handful of pending requests were awaiting a first response - mostly labelled urgent, clients always believed their case was urgent - which he ignored for now and opened his current case. Filed under the Rearden account, he re-read the file notes for last night's case, and dug out the images he had managed to capture before the contact had been stolen, there were no unauthorised accesses to his storage at least. At least they hadn't corrupted. He hoped the pay day would be worth the bruises.

The coffee machine hissed and Ryoma poured himself a cup, feeling its warmth soak into his hands. People always complained about his hands; organic and synthetic, they were both too cold.

He stood by the window watching the ships taking off from the port, willing the throbbing behind his eye to disappear, trying to think through the case. People had reacted badly to being investigated before, but this seemed like something else. The handover he'd seen burrowed into his brain. He should easily end it there; a guy seemingly flirting with another woman on some party planet was exactly what the client had wanted. Maybe it was his sister's influence; Serena had said he'd had a nose for these things, that he could tell from the way people moved. But he needed someone he could talk it through with, and she wasn't around anymore. He'd need to phone a friend, if they even wanted to hear from him, that is.

The screen flickered. That woman in the Satellite bar had come up blank on every search he could think of, which was suspicious in itself. He'd need someone with better access to the net, maybe she was a blank. A name sprang to mind, one of his sister's old friends and an expert in all things related to synths across the Outer System. But he wasn't sure she'd want to talk. Last time they'd seen each other he'd been in a particularly deep well of grief, trying to make sense of Serena's death, largely angry at himself, and hadn't been the best company. In general Ryoma found friends were thin on the ground, most had known him by proxy with Serena, and once she was gone they seemed to fall away. Casual friendships had never come easily to him. Flirting was easy enough, people liked his honesty, but much longer than that, he found himself feeling increasingly in the way and quietly disappeared from their lives. The closest he'd gotten was Sylph Ochoa.

His hand hovered over the call button for a second, wondering what the time difference would be, if this was an inopportune time to call. Not that she slept, to his knowledge. She didn't need to. Tapping the screen anyway, he watched as the tinny speaker hummed tunelessly and half hoped she wouldn't pick up. He could continue alone. Abruptly, the ring cut off, replaced with the light clattering of someone unprepared for a call.

"Sylph? It's me. It's uh, Serena's brother." Belatedly, he peeled off the tape covering the camera on his device, hurrying to make himself presentable, pushing his hair back and finishing the buttons on his shirt. Whilst he waited for the response he found himself staring at the miniature version of himself on the screen. He looked tired as all hell, but it could be worse.

"Ryo?" He snapped to attention when her voice broke through after a delay of a minute or so. She couldn't be too far away, within the system at least. Her camera flicked on belatedly, and his old friend popped into view, the screen glow giving her dark skin an ethereal shimmer. She hadn't aged a day since they had met. The woman looked incredulously at her screen. "It's been a long time, haven't seen you since..."

"Yeah. I know." Ryoma, uncomfortable with the reminder, rifled through the dresser for a cigarette but came up empty. He'd shown up drunk to the memorial.

She cocked an eyebrow at his snappiness. "You look like shit Ryo, where have you been?"

"All around," he said vaguely, he couldn't always remember if he was honest. Aware of the raspiness in his voice, he paused for a sip. "I'm on Scylla at the moment."

Sylph snorted derisively. "That tourist trap? Maxed out your credit in a shitty casino yet?"

"Not quite, although my wallet's feeling light. " He shrugged, warming to the conversation, maybe he should call more often. They'd been pretty close before. "I was working actually."

She leaned back in her chair and whistled. "All the way out there? They must be a pretty beautiful client for you to trudge out to that tacky shithole."

"Ha ha," he said dryly. "Should be a pretty good pay actually, I think she's hoping to pay me from the divorce settlement. Last I heard you'd gone underground after that server leak from NachtCorp, I'm assuming that was you."

"I wouldn't know anything about that. Ryo." Her lip twisted. "A remote break-in on the servers for one of the most powerful corps in the system? You'd have to be insane. But that's what they get I suppose. Holding people's bodies for ransom like that."

Yeah, that's what I thought.

"I'm on Polaris for the time being, I'm aiming for a spot on a generation ship. I figured it'd be easy to get on the crew, synths don't need cryo. I'd like to see what's out there, in the deep. I think I've seen enough of what they're offering around here."

"That's, that's great." His heart sank with the feeling of one more person slipping away. "You'll see a lot out there."

"Let's hope." She shifted in her seat. "So what did you call me for, 'cause it wasn't just to say hi."

"You've really got me down huh?" He cracked a smile. "I was wondering if you could do me a favour, if you still have the access you used to have to the net, the hive. Whatever you call it."

There was no point being coy. Subtlety wasn't his strong point, nor were computers. In the past he'd defaulted to Sylph's expertise where needed, but it had been a while. There was a pause, just long enough for Ryo to think the call had been dropped, severed by a momentary blip or perhaps Sylph had grown tired of him.

"Is this line secure?"

"Secure enough." He shrugged, Scylla's independence meant it was beholden to no one, so he sent the case notes through anyway. "I'll send over what I've got."

"You got some big case in the works? Someone famous get jacked or something?"

"No nothing like that, but...I don't know, something doesn't sit right with this one. Well, a few things actually."

He felt Sylph peering at him through the screen, with those synthetic eyes he probably looked a lot worse, every pore and burst blood vessel clear as day. "You look pretty beat up, Ryo. Shit, you didn't take up fighting again for the extra credits, did you?"

"Nothing like that." Ryoma had always felt in the back of his mind like he'd kept relatively fit since retiring, but if last night had proved anything, his reactions were shot to pieces. Before he could see everything in how his opponent moved, measuring the distance, the weight in their swing. Last night he'd seen nothing except his own weakness. "The office is gone, couldn't pay by myself. I work out of my apartment now."

He felt a guilty pang in his gut for letting the office go. It had been modest, they'd made use of the space well, pouring whatever credits they could into a professional looking space to attract the more monied clients. But with Serena gone he hadn't been able to take on the caseload they had as a pair, and any credits he'd had saved had quickly dwindled to nothing. The locks had been changed one night, and he'd had to break in to retrieve what little he could.

"Shit, sorry Ryo. You should have said something, we could have..."

"It's fine, really." Ryoma shrugged, unsure why he lied. "Concerning this case, well you'll see actually."

At that, the woman turned to look at a screen to her left, exposing a shimmering silver seam wrapped around her ear, something every full-body synth seemed to have. Sylph had tried to explain the mechanics to him once but he'd glazed over when she started explaining how they related to the function of synaptic contact gel. She hummed lightly as she skimmed through the raw footage of the previous night until she winced, eyes glancing back at him. "Shit Ryo, I see what you mean."

"A pretty rough warning, right? I think I might have seen something I shouldn't, maybe in that bar." He tried to play it down, not to feel the shame in showing her his humiliation.

"You shouldn't be working alone on cases, Ryo. You need backup at least, at least on an independent like Scylla. Are you alright?"

"Worse for wear, but alive." He leaned forward to show off the pale scar above his eye and internally debated if he should tell her about his rescuer but he decided to keep it to himself for now. "Thought maybe you could do some digging where I wouldn't think to look, give me some insight. Maybe you can find out who that woman in the bar was, I got a decent look. But there's nothing in the ID centres, not even work registration."

"In the blue?" She glanced at the screen again, rolling the thought in her mind. They'd been good friends once, Ryoma hoped he hadn't burnt too much good will these past years. "I'll see what I can do, anything for Serena's bro right?"

"Yeah." He smiled, relieved. The possibility of a challenge was too much it seemed.

She grinned and held up a finger. "But! Only if you promise I'll see you soon. I think you owe me a drink for this. And we need a catch up. A real one. I've missed you, man."

"Sure thing, Syl. I'll be back on Polaris in about thirty hours. The client's pretty eager for me to hand over anything at all. I don't think she's even interested in the particulars."

"Sounds like she's in a hurry to cut loose. Well, I'll see you around, dragon boy." She winked and hung up before he could protest. It had been borderline ironic when he'd been boxing but now it just made him feel old.

"Boy? I'll be forty in," he checked the standard date on his wrist and kissed his teeth. "A month, fuck."

He slumped back in the chair, looking around at the mess he'd made of the motel room over the last few days. He needed help.

Chapter Five

"**S**is, what are we doing here?"

Ryoma glanced nervously through the large windowed office doors, the silhouettes of a lot of upper-city types milled around through the frosted glass. There's no way the two of them belonged here, two rock hoppers from the belt, and he was sure everyone knew it. He half expected a corp enforcer to appear and remove them from the building, but Serena seemed confident nonetheless. She was far more chameleonic in her appearance than he ever was, following trends closely enough she could fit into any part of the city no problem.

Ryoma followed his twin with a slouch, his body still aching from last night's fight, his ribs and jaw radiating low level pain that stims couldn't quite cover. Fighting heavily modded guys was tough but it paid better. People liked an underdog, steel vs. flesh, even with his arm. The winnings would keep him fed for a month or so, if he was careful, which he often wasn't.

"Come on. I want to show you something." Serena stopped at the end of the corridor and began searching her jacket pockets, producing a fresh keycard amongst some crumpled credit notes and ticket stubs. The door slid open into a small but brightly lit space, with high ceilings and washed out green walls where the lack of blinds had baked the room dry under the oppressive glare of the suns.

"What do you think, Ry?" She whirled around, her earrings clinking as they fought to keep up her momentum. Her excited voice echoed in the hollow space, the soles of her well-worn boots clicking on the floor.

"It's pretty rough around the edges."

"Says you." She looked at him sharply. He'd walked right into that. "It just needs a little love, that's all. It was a steal too, cheapest unit in the block by far."

"I can see why." He chuckled and ran his nail against the wall, peeling up a few loose chips of paint. It needed a lot of love, but maybe it could be something. "But, it's a good spot if you want access to the Upper."

"That's the idea, you can see it from here. You still shacked up with, uh what was their name?"

"Warren. And no." He let his hand drop and sighed. "Sort of fucked things up, actually."

"Again?" She asked, incredulous but not unsympathetic. They'd asked him to move in and he'd baulked at the idea of living uptown, another place he didn't belong.

"Again."

Again.

He coughed and looked around. "So, what is this all for?"

"This is the office for LeBeau Investigations. Well, it will be. The previous tenant was nice enough to leave most of the furniture too. Said they got a ticket out to the deep and didn't need it anymore. Pretty good since I don't think I could afford it after paying the deposit."

"Using the family name huh? You're really serious about this thing." Ryoma collapsed onto the well-loved sofa in the middle of the room, the aches from the previous night baring down on him, and ran his fingers along cracked pleather. The idea of a detective agency had been on her mind for a long time, but he'd always thought it was just a pipedream from watching too many movies. "You really think you could make a difference here?"

"Don't see why not, Ry. We just got to get a few uptown clients to pay the bills, get some business cards printed to look legit, then we can work cheap or free in the Under. Work out a sliding scale or something." She walked over to the window and heaved it open with some effort, letting in a warm breeze. Neither of them had quite got used to the heat of the twin suns even after a decade on-world. She looked down at the city below. "Better than doing nothing."

"We? Is Sylph working with you?" It wasn't a bad idea. The two of them together could solve half the system's problems if no one stopped them.

"No, Sylph is... well you know her." She turned inward and sat on the window sill. His own eyes mirrored back at him. "I was hoping you could, actually."

Ryoma scoffed. "What good would I be?"

"It'd be steady work. Better than fighting until your body gives out." Serena had never liked his fighting, but he was no good at anything else. He was just a body. "You're gonna get yourself really hurt one of these days, Ryo."

"I don't need looking after sis." He sat up and fiddled with his lighter, his synthetic knuckles were scuffed, the organic ones were bruised and split.

"I know that, you ass." She sighed, visibly frustrated. "What I meant is I hardly see you anymore. We were gonna do this together, weren't we? Take on Polaris, the two of us.

"Yeah. We were." Ryoma felt the tension from his shoulders unravel. He wondered how many fights he had left in him. "Do you still miss home?"

"Yeah, sometimes." Serena looked up at the twin suns burning above them. "Do you remember the rain?"

"I can still hear it some nights." It had been raining the day they left, the whole exoplanet cracked a few days later. Just dust now. Maybe there was some stability to be found here. "I'll think about it, the detective thing."

Chapter Six

The ship headed home was abuzz with a mixture of commuters and tourists whose luck had run out. The bar was already open when he boarded the vast commercial ship, and Ryoma was half-way tempted until he saw the price list. He needed a clear head anyway. Ignoring his reserved seat, Ryoma looked for a quiet spot by the engine room and took a cat nap. The low-level drone of the drive was unpleasant for most, but he found it as soothing as any white noise. He dozed for a few hours, dreaming of cool, comforting hands and strange old music until he was jolted awake by the ship entering the thick polluted atmosphere of Polaris northern central. He made his way to one of the exits, ready to disembark as soon as possible, and peered out of the window. It was evening already, the city below had taken on a gloomy amber glow amongst the dark greys and blues of the skyscrapers, clustered tightly on the landmass.

Stepping off the ship, he took in a lung of cool air, clearing out the warm recycled air he'd been surviving on for days. His apartment wasn't far and he needed to save the credits where he could, so he decided to walk. The doors of the 'port opened out into a bustling city, too loud and packed, the towering buildings of the hub city making him immediately claustrophobic and tense. Slipping down a side street by one of the better regarded VR suites, he made his way towards the far older part of the city. Soon, the bustle of excited tourists visiting the system's capital and upper echelons that lived there gave way to the loose communities that occupied the oldest parts of the Under. It was hoped that leaving it unattended with no funds or corp security to speak of, would lead to its eventual collapse but it had only grown over the years. Ryoma and Serena had ended up there when they arrived on the planet as teens along with many others from failed colonies who were wary of corp work. People could fall through the system easily there, which is just how he liked it.

"Ryo, you're back!"

It took him a second to recognise his old sparring partner, maybe he was still a bit concussed. "Oh dude, you look like shit, you start fighting again?"

"Thanks, Alto." He barely slowed his pace, thinking of nothing but taking a decent night's sleep.

Alto continued to follow despite Ryoma's purposeful stride, looking him up and down with a slow appreciation. "Drink sometime? It's been a while."

Not now.

"Sure, maybe." It was never just drinks.

Alto continued to chatter away telling him about his work venture, running as a heavy for some corporate type from uptown paranoid enough to think they need protection. Ryoma remained virtually silent, hoping the message would sink in that he wasn't in the mood. His brain was fried and he just needed some quiet to think. Mercifully, he quickly reached his building where they parted ways, agreeing to drinks and all that implied, making a mental note to find some reason to cancel.

Ryoma slumped against the wall of the elevator in blessed silence, waiting for it to sluggishly carry him to the upper third of the tower block. The tight clusters of buildings gave way to traffic, and the mist clung to the outside as droplets, and then eventually just the sky, tinted grey by the sun shields on the glass. Home.

With a little persuading, Ryoma's keycard flickered green and unlocked, all the exhaustion hitting him at once. He threw the borrowed shirt onto the laundry heap, then immediately changed his mind and folded the delicate fabric carefully, thinking of Guin again. Faintly, he hoped that maybe they'd swing by, and he'd have an excuse to invite them in. Maybe for a drink, maybe more. He'd left his card after all, they'd only need to call to find him. Desire pooled in his gut.

Distracted again.

There was nothing Ryoma wanted more than to hibernate until his body recovered but he still had to report back to his client. Pulling on a fresh shirt, he switched on the agency tablet. Notifications pinged and flashed, alerting him once again of the backlog of prospective clients and payments that needed chasing. He didn't like to chase, it made him feel like a debt collector. He was about to get to work when the screen flashed with an incoming call, the caller ID identifying 'E. R.' She'd been awaiting an update, and Ryoma didn't exactly help when he made himself uncontactable for days at a time.

Quickly, he placed it on his coffee table to face the cleanest part of the apartment, a blank wall that he tried to keep free of junk to at least give the illusion he had a real office. The video feed flickered on, and Elise Rearden appeared, plucked eyebrows raised at his appearance. The scarring on his forehead needed another week or two before it settled.

"Morning Ms Rearden." He tried not to sound too sheepish, he was a professional after all.

"It's been a week Mr. LeBeau, I've been trying to contact you." The woman sat stiffly almost posing, peering over the collar of her silver overcoat, eyes eager for information.

"Apologies, it ain't... uh it took a little more time than I expected to track him." He responded, trying to flatten his accent out when she wrinkled her nose. That 'rock hopper lilt', Guin had endearingly called it.

"But you found something? Correct? He's seeing someone else." Her gaze kept shifting to the left. He imagined she was waiting to push through the separation documents as soon as he confirmed anything, hand hovering over the send button on a screen.

"I can't say for sure, I could do with a little more time to check some things." With what he had, it definitely *looked* that way, but something still gnawed at him. It sure seemed like she'd made her decision about what he was up to already. He could just hand over all the what he had and be done with it, the rest was just his own curiosity.

"You don't know *for sure?* So you did see something?" She looked at him keenly through the feed. All Ryoma wanted was to lie down for a few days to sleep off the ache and embarrassment, but that wouldn't happen until he sent Elise something.

"Fuck it," he mumbled. "Sure I saw him with someone, I don't have an ID, which is why I'd like more time to confirm but..."

"I'll take what you have," she said sharply.

"You're the boss lady." He scanned over his notes one last time before he finally attached the extremely trimmed footage and sent it across. "It was this dive bar on Scylla, I didn't recognise the woman but... "

"The fucker." The mask slipped for just a second, her cleanly neutral expression spilled into a mix of fury and joy. Someone she recognised? "You'll have to excuse me. You'll get your payment momentarily Mr. LeBeau, I'd say it was a pleasure doing business, but..."

The feed cut off abruptly, leaving Ryoma looking at his own reflection, feeling hollow, and just a little slimier than before.

Another case for the pile, sis.

He'd been working flat out since Serena died, needled by the feeling that if he stopped everything would just fall apart. But the last day or so had shown he desperately needed to rest. He was getting sloppy, making mistakes that got him hurt, the next one could leave him dead.

The screen bleeped to indicate a payment was processing, at least she was quick about it. Ryoma was ready to rid himself of the case, except... The image of that drive being illicitly passed over wormed away at the back of his mind. It was a loose thread, and he couldn't not pull on it, he could never leave well enough alone. Maybe Sylph would turn up something on this woman, that would be a start. Even just to sate his own curiosity.

Still, his mind was already wandering back to the other night, those gentle hands taking care of him, the reassuring hum of their voice.

What was the name of that bar again?

Chapter Seven

The Reinhardt was a bar built on anachronism. The polished white exterior quickly gave way to an entirely different interior, imported wholesale from the past, or at least someone's idea of it. Through to the main floor from the reception there was a heavily decorated bar and seating area, a handful of plush crimson booths, trimmed with gold, occupying a space that could easily seat many more. A waiter was milling around dressed in a similar style to Guin had when they'd met; although in his opinion it had suited them a lot better.

"Do you have a reservation sir?" A highly strung voice called from the front desk. As he approached the woman spoke again. Her hair clung to her scalp in shiny waves, a loose sequined dress hung from her shoulders. "We're fully booked out tonight."

"I was hoping to see someone, uh, Guin?" The woman seemed unmoved, perhaps he was saying it wrong.

"Are you on the list?" Ryoma felt himself being examined, he got the feeling he wasn't the usual clientele. Her eyes lingered on his scuffed shoes and his open necked shirt. He'd clearly committed some faux pas, at least in her eyes.

"Well I ain't, but..." He felt a door closing on him and helplessly he wondered if maybe Guin had lied, just to get rid of him.

"Then we're booked out, Sir." The woman said firmly, her eyes darting up. "You'll have to leave, we're opening soon."

"He's a friend, Neve." A familiar voice sounded as he turned, Guin had appeared soundlessly behind him, immaculately dressed in a waistcoat and tie. They turned their attention to Ryo. "Come through here, I'll find space for you."

"A friend? That's a first for you." Neve remarked, well within earshot, as Ryoma was led through the seating area and past what looked like a very well stocked bar; some of it even looked Terran. The import fees alone on a bottle would bankrupt most.

"Your co-workers seem pleasant."

"I'm afraid Neve's somewhat of a purist, your shirt isn't period accurate." The smile in their voice was audible.

The pair passed the brightly lit raised stage, where a few other musicians were tuning their instruments. The piano, a glittering glass baby grand, remained notably unoccupied. Guin nodded at them as they passed, and Ryoma felt a few more sets of eyes follow him. Through a door to the side of the stage, the glamour quickly faded back to the metallic industrial interior, the opulent warmth replaced with the chilled ozone fragrance of air recyclers and the voices of the other staff becoming wordless echoes. Guin led him into a cramped room, little more than a cupboard with a dressing table and a small rail of suits and dresses that took up most of the floor.

"Your own room? You must be the star of the show."

"Here, hold on." Guin cleared some loose makeup brushes and palettes to one side and perched on the dressing table, offering him the only seat. "Please?"

"Thank you."

"I saw you lingering in the entrance, trying to wrangle with Neve. Guess you couldn't stay away, huh?"

"Couldn't stay away." He agreed. "Look, I didn't mean to lurk or nothing. I just wanted to see what my nurse's day job was like, is all."

He neglected to mention he'd come back especially for them, that would make him look even more like...

Like a pervert.

"Well, here I am, in my natural habitat." Guin towered over him in the small, intimate room. "How are you feeling Ryo? You need a tune up?"

"No, no, I'm fine. I was curious about your act, actually. This place is a little... old fashioned. I knew your uniform was strange but I didn't expect the whole bar to be themed so intricately."

"It's a bit of a novelty I suppose, but I like the style." They adjusted the tie around their throat in the mirror, checking their hair. They frowned, and Ryoma felt himself being observed again, but this time under Guin's more sympathetic eye. "Your arm still looks a little stiff, are you sure you don't need anything?"

"Uh, it aches, but it's fine. I'm still pretty sore all over." He flexed his hand to reassure them, though he was flattered that they cared. He wondered if they'd thought of him too. "That's a pretty good spot. You'd make a pretty good detective yourself, you know?"

"I don't know about that." They smiled modestly, one corner of their mouth raising a little more than the other. "I just like watching people, and I can do that a lot around here, a lot of folks passing through. Making friends can be a little hard around here, so I take what I can get."

"It's a good skill to have. You know I could always do with an assistant, if you've got the time." There was a lull, the pair looking at each other quietly.

Say something you idiot.

"Guin, I wanted -"

"River you're - , oh uh, excuse me sir, I didn't see you there." A voice stiffly cut through their conversation, seemingly surprised by the guest in their dressing room, they must not get too many visitors. The floor manager was a nervous looking man, his suit clung to his frame awkwardly, like it was made for someone else. "You're on in ten, have you got the setlist?"

"Of course." Guin nodded, their eyes darted to Ryoma's. "I'll be there in a minute."

"River?" He repeated as the man walked away. A false name? "That'll be why I got blank looks when I asked for you."

"It's a stage name, of sorts. With the kind of music I play, Moon River, Cry Me a River... I needed a change and it felt like it suited me. If that makes sense." Ryoma got the feeling they were imparting more than they meant to. They checked their appearance once more in the mirror, watching him in the reflection. "Will you stay and watch? I'd very much like it if you did."

"I'd love to."

"Thank you." Guin smiled and opened the door leading him back through the cramped corridor to the cavernous golden club floor. Guin hailed a waiter to serve him a drink, promptly disappeared into the back to prepare.

The receptionist wasn't lying when she said it was booked out, the booths had completely filled in the short time they'd spoken. Half the people seated were recognisable to anyone with a passing knowledge of the outer system. Synthetics and mining oligarchs, shipping magnates, emperors of their own little kingdoms. A who's who of the unfathomably wealthy, all with their accompanying entourages. Ryoma wondered if any of them needed a problem looked into, he could charge a small fortune in expenses and they'd barely notice.

Feeling vastly out of place, Ryoma remained steadfast at the bar, and ordered a measure of whatever looked cheapest. He'd have to dress up if he wanted to fit in around here. At least he had a good view of the stage.

It occurred to him he'd never asked what exactly they played, when the lights dimmed into near darkness and the band appeared from behind the heavy crimson curtains all similarly dressed. He'd find out soon enough. Although there were several other musicians in the band, Ryoma looked only at Guin, their tie now perfectly centred and hair hung loose to frame their face just so. He watched them take a seat at the gleaming transparent piano, and turn subtly to look into the awaiting audience, to look for him, he hoped. There was a slight rumble as the band warmed up and they began to play.

He didn't know an awful lot about music, it was something he mainly used as background noise when he was busy, something to fill the silence, like any other sort of white noise.

But the ease with which Guin played was impressive, their hands gliding along the keys, melody perfectly threading through the sound of each instrument and weaving them together. The insides of the piano danced to their tune, the orange glow of the lowered lighting illuminating the instrument with warmth.

When they began to sing, a part of him cracked open. Their speaking voice was gentle, a little practised even, but their singing voice shed that entirely. Far warmer, a little deeper than he expected, and deeply sad.

The music they played was old, it had been old before the settlement of the outer system was even a dream, but their voice carried it across the centuries to an ungrateful audience. Most of the crowd were barely paying attention, talking and drinking, wrapped up in their own worlds. Guin's beauty was mere background noise to them. They spoke very briefly between songs, introducing the song title and little more; from the audience Ryoma couldn't help but wonder if their lips were as soft as they looked. More than once they seemed to be looking right at him, smiling just barely as their voice captured the sense of loss he'd spent almost four years trying to verbalise.

Their set ended to a smattering of polite applause, far too soon for Ryoma's liking. As the band disappeared backstage, he felt a wave of melancholy hit him. He felt alone, but trying to get backstage to see Guin felt pathetic and finished his drink, the whiskey burning in the pit of his stomach. He quickly paid his tab, alarmingly expensive for a single measure, and headed outside.

Feeling strangely frustrated, he lit a cigarette; a habit he'd never quite shaken, despite the efforts of just about everyone he knew. Especially his sister. The evening chill bit into him as he wandered the district aimlessly, in search of somewhere to kill time until he was exhausted. The motel would be just another empty room. He sighed, wondering what the hell he was even doing, following a pretty stranger around like a stray dog.

Pathetic old man. What would they want with you?

He raised his hand to call down a taxi and bundled himself in, their songs still echoing in his mind.

"Where to?" The taxi's AI asked, when he didn't immediately bark a destination into the speaker.

"I don't know, somewhere distracting." The taxi clicked, processing his vague request and then took off silently.

Chapter Eight

Ryoma found himself further down the main strip, in front of the flashiest of the casinos on the rock, the Platinum. The hotel was exclusive, but the casino would take anyone willing to pay. He clucked his tongue as he paid his fare, damn thing was probably programmed to drop people there. Inside, every surface was slick with gleaming black and silver. The steady white lights over the busy tables created a surreal parody of modernity in stark contrast to the half remembered past of the Reinhardt.

The noise of simultaneous wins and losses (and there were definitely more of one than the other), were an assault on the senses that set Ryoma on edge, so he made straight for the bar. Quietly ordering a drink, he looked around for the best place to fritter his well-earned fee away. Roulette seemed quiet, tucked at the back of the darkened main hall, with a single blue light hanging over the table. It wouldn't be the worst way he'd spent an evening. With a sizable lump of his credit transferred into chips, he approached the table and tried his luck.

"Uh, outside low," he said, pushing a few chips into the table. Not a sure bet, but safe enough.

"Outside low sir," the croupier confirmed, and set the wheel spinning.

Ryoma leaned against the table and watched closely as the pockets flickered in alternate white and cool blues as the ball passed by them, rapidly at first and then slowing until it clattered into its resting place.

Damn.

"Bad luck, sir." The stack of chips was swiftly swept away from Ryoma, and watching them, he felt his resolve harden, the belief he could win it back crept up on him. It wasn't like he had anything else to do. "Another?"

He nodded, watching the wheel spin a few more times, losing track of time. His credits weren't going as far as he'd like. The minimum bet was high, though he suspected that was the intention of the house, to keep undesirables out. At least they let him smoke inside. He wondered if there was a way he could change up a few more credits, slip this into Elise Rearden's bill as a business expense. Surely he could spin a tale of tracking Dayne across the casinos of Scylla, having to maintain cover.

Before he knew it, he was standing, rubbing his final two chips together, staring at the table considering just one last round. There was nowhere else to go but back to his motel room, maybe he could pick someone up on the way, but he wasn't in the mood to flirt tonight. At least not with anyone else. Maybe he'd just go back to his room and let his mind and hands wander just to get the thought of them out of his system. Bend the memory of their voice into something pornographic. At least then he could write this trip off as an embarrassing flight of fancy, and get back to normal.

"Ryo?" He jolted at the sound of his name so close. Guin. It was like he'd summoned them with a thought.

"You found me." He tried not to sound too enamoured, thinking about them chasing after him. "You're quite the tracker."

"When I didn't see you during the second set, I looked for you. The door guy said he saw heading this way." They reached out, just themself stopping short of touching his wrist, as though thinking better of it and looked curiously at his paltry pile of chips. "Was the music not your thing?"

"No, no I loved it, I..." His throat felt raw. "You didn't say you could sing."

"Oh," they smiled apprehensively, clearly confused. "I guessed that was a given when I said that I played."

"Yeah, I guess so."

They fingered the knot in their tie until it hung loose, and eyed what was in his hand. "Not so lucky tonight either huh?"

"Doesn't seem that way, though I much prefer this than being kicked to shit in an alley somewhere." Ryoma laughed dryly and took the crumpled box from his back pocket to offer them a cigarette but it came up empty. He looked at the heaping ashtray that had been silently placed next to him at some point during the evening. "Shit. Sorry"

"That's ok, it doesn't do much for me." Odd way to phrase it, he thought. "Well, I'm free for the rest of the night. If you want another drink, I know a good place. Cheaper than the Reinhardt too, that place you're paying for the theme really. And the drinks here are watered down." They nodded in the direction of the sleekly designed pearlescent bar.

"I thought as such, Belter's Brew usually got more of a kick to it. So..." A smile crept across his lips as he looked up at them, trying not to appear too smug. "You're asking me out?"

"We were cut short earlier, I thought maybe we could pick up where we left off. If you like. When you left, I wondered if maybe you were just being polite, showing an interest like that." They'd thought the exact same thing about him.

"No I, I just needed some air, and I guess I got a little distracted, my mind wanders sometimes."

Wanders to the other side of the city.

"So where's this bar?"

"Not far, just a few minutes walk." They nodded towards the exit, then waved to the croupier, who had taken a polite step back whilst they spoke. "Uh, he'll put it all on thirty-three blue please."

"Straight thirty three, yessirs," he said with an almost military beat, pushing the meagre stack across the table.

The wheel spun one last time, the ball skittering a few times across the edges of the pockets, causing the lights to illuminate erratically, before landing with a rattle. Thirty-three blue.

"Well done sirs."

"Huh. You must be my lucky charm." Ryoma stared dumbfounded at the neat stack of high value chips being pushed toward him. Picking up a couple, he turned them over in his hand, a pale translucent pink, embossed and etched. He'd never held this much money before. "Maybe I should keep you around."

"Maybe you should." Their eyes darted around as they spoke, looking uneasy. "I'm not really allowed in here, we better cash in quick."

"Oh uh, sure." He stood, cupped the chips in one hand and headed towards the cashier. He slapped them down with a dramatic rattle, and held out his wrist for credit transfer, his mind racing as he tried to calculate how long he could make this last. "You get caught counting cards or something?"

"Something like that," they said quietly, head bowed to avoid facing the near ubiquitous scanners that seemed to be everywhere

Ryoma whistled as the credits transferred over to his account, the healthy number of zeros on the balance on his wrist indicated rent was sorted for the next couple of months. "So what bar was this? I must owe you a second drink by now. At least."

"It's across town near the 'port. It's not as... polished as here, but it's got its charms. I think it might be your thing."

"Sure, darling. Lead the way."

The crowded main strip eventually thinned out as they made their way through the quiet back streets. Ryoma had his suspicions about where they were going but he said nothing, playing innocent for now. Eventually they rounded a corner and he was met with a familiar pink sign, The Satellite. He even spotted the doorway where he'd sheltered from the rain, those were the cigarette butts he'd dropped too. Street cleaning must not come this far away from the tourist district.

"It's a little out of the way, but it's fairly homely, for a rock like this I mean. And I know the bartender." Guin opened the door, letting Ryoma enter first. It was far quieter than it had been on his previous visit, almost cosy with its warm light and low level chatter creating a pleasant background buzz.

"So that's what you got up to." Immediately, Ryoma recognised the honeyed voice that called as they approached the bar. The bartender grinned at his embarrassment, the same neatly dressed pretty boy as the other night. "Whiskey, no ice, right?"

Guin looked between the two wordlessly

"Yeah," Ryoma said sheepishly. "That's right."

"Vodka for me, Autumn," Guin said without skipping a beat. They ran a hand through their hair, dark strands catching the light. Ryoma noticed something else there too, something silver.

"Coming right up," Autumn turned around, suppressing a grin.

"I was here the other night, just before I met you actually. We got talking, must have hit it off." Ryoma didn't know why he was scrambling to explain himself, he'd done nothing wrong, but still he felt a smattering of shame.

Guin smirked, leaning into his shoulder. "I can see that. Aut's got a thing for tough guys, you're definitely his type."

"Yeah? I didn't feel so tough by the end of the night." He leaned back, letting the bar take his weight as he relaxed. Something about their presence set him at ease.

"You seem like you've bounced back pretty well." Were they flirting? It felt like it.

"Your expert care did most of the work."

Guin opened their mouth to retort, but a polite cough broke their flow.

"If I could interrupt?" The bartender winked at them both, placing the drinks on the bar. "Have fun you two."

Guin thanked him, looking flustered, and took their drink. "Let's sit down."

"That voice of yours, I've never heard anything like it," Ryoma said as he made a beeline for a booth towards the back, and realised he was next to where he'd seen Rearden and his compatriot. He expected Guin to politely sit opposite but pleasantly surprised when they perched next to him, idly stirring their drink with a slender finger.

Flirt.

"Thank you. It's lovely music isn't it? I heard it when I was young and I've loved it ever since. It's pretty good work to be a singer who never loses their voice." That final point stuck to his mind as they talked, he remembered how strong they'd been that night, their intimate knowledge of synthetics. Pieces falling into place.

"You're a synth, aren't you?" He asked, a little more abruptly than he meant to. "I mean, I think I saw your contact seam."

They smiled, pushing back their hair to show off the silver seam that coiled behind their ear. "You've got a good eye, full body and all."

There was a pearlescent sheen to the surface, like the inside of a shell. He knew they'd have a similar seam snaking all the way down their back from their neck, to just above their ass. He cleared his throat and tried to push the image out of his mind as they continued.

"Brain's mostly organic, some of my spine but that's it." They let their hair fall back in place, black silk shimmered about their chin. "You aren't going to ask why I'm like this?"

"Don't see why I should," he shrugged into his drink. "There's all sorts of folks, not really my place to interrogate."

"Thank you." He knew that sting of being questioned about his body, leered and prodded at. Putting anyone else through that seemed unkind at best. "That's why I had to hustle you out of the casino pretty sharp like. The corps that run those places think anyone with a jot of brainwork is gonna strip the house bare, counting cards or hustling the machines. Still, Scylla's not the worst place for someone like me."

"People can be shitty about what they don't know." A look of recognition passed between them. "Say, how'd you know it was such a sure bet? Back there on the tables?"

"There was a slight incline, barely perceptible if their own people haven't noticed it. The bet I placed was just slightly more likely than others. So maybe they are right." They winked cheekily. "But what would I do with it?"

"I'm sure you'd find a use for a few credits, if that's how easily you win."

"I suppose, although if I get caught winning I don't think they'd let me stick around. Not sure where I'd go from here, where I'd sing." They ran their fingers along the table, stamped with the texture of wood grain. Ryoma wondered if this little lump of rock had ever seen a tree.

"I'd hate for you to lose that. Didn't understand a lot of it but..." He stumbled on his words, frustrated, he was normally far more loquacious. At least he thought so. "It was really something."

"Thank you. The language is an older Terran dialect, and people seem to like that Old World thing. They've kept me around for a good few seasons now, much longer than most, so I can't be too bad." They looked wistfully into nothing, just for a moment. "I'm being rude aren't I? I've hardly asked about you. How did you get into detective work? There seems to be a fair few of those around these days."

"Well it's not like there's law enforcement around, unless you do something to piss off colony admins, or the corps that own them. Regular people need help sometimes. Started a while back with my sister actually, built up a decent rep, mainly her doing of course. She's the brains of the operation really," he said, not bothering to correct himself.

"The brains. What does that make you? The brawn, the beauty?"

"I don't think that's how that saying goes darling." He stared into his drink trying to suppress a laugh. "I don't really like to talk shop too much when I'm not working."

"Sure, of course, it must be intense. You've got to switch off sometimes." Their gaze shifted down to his silver hand, he noticed they'd seemed intrigued the other night too. "Have you got other synthetics? If you don't mind me asking."

"It's just the arm, and that busted contact lens I suppose. The arm itself is old, but it works. Just like me, I reckon." Looking at the scuffs and dings all over his hand, Ryoma began to feel oddly imperfect, sitting next to someone so carefully, beautifully engineered. "I guess I must seem like a luddite to you, all flesh and bone. Aches and pains."

"Not at all, the technology works for you, not the other way around, you use what you need." Guin inclined their head, their gaze soft. "That lizard you've got is pretty. I've seen a lot of custom work but I've rarely seen such delicate engraving like that before, who did it?"

He rubbed his wrist, thoughts drifting. "That was my sister too actually. Etched it a few years ago for a birthday, it was her design."

"That's a beautiful gift, you must be close. Is she here too?"

He looked at them blankly for a second, and for a moment he thought maybe she was still around, out doing the hard work whilst he schmoozes with the locals.

"No, she's ... it's just me now." His throat tightened and he felt the mood shift. Guin shrank back in their seat. Message received.

"I'm so sorry."

"It's fine, really." Ryoma shrugged and finished his drink with a gulp. It wasn't a thought he wanted to linger on. "So, you normally pick up strays off the street?"

They shook their head, a little more tentative. "You're the first. To be honest, I thought you were just passed out drunk till I noticed how cut up you were. It can get kind of rough around here, especially to tourists who don't expect it."

"Yeah."

"That said, they don't often come back. Have you got a taste for Old World jazz standards, or are you hoping to get lucky at the Platinum, or...?"

"Like I said, I was curious about you." He figured he might as well be honest, they seemed to appreciate that quality. "Ain't listened to that sort of music much before but, I think I'm beginning to see the appeal. Especially if the singers look like you."

"You liked me that much huh?" They gazed coyly into their drink. "You're very forward aren't you, Ryo."

"Guess I am." He'd never been one to hold back on someone he liked the look of, and it had served him well, most of the time. "You don't mind?"

"You don't play games." They leaned slightly toward him, chin in hand. "It's cute."

"I know what I like." His gaze shifted across and downward, catching sight of the edges of a tattoo on their chest in the shadows of their shirt. It was too distorted from that angle to make out what it was, but he could have sworn there was a soft glow in there. His mind wandered as they spoke, idly wondering what the rest of it looked like, and how far down it went.

The pair worked their way down the menu, Guin watched him intently as he spoke, asking him about his trips to Scylla and life on Polaris. He felt his initial anxiety melt away and his tongue loosen. In return, they spoke in soft intones about their music practice, that they'd picked up their mechanical skills over the years of doing minor work on themself. Something of an expert it seemed.

"You've got to know the basics out here, anyone licensed will charge you an arm and leg, proverbially speaking, and that's if they'll work on a synth from 'Phaestus at all."

"Hephaestus? That colony that got bought out way back?" He remembered hearing people talking about it as a child, the forge colony that tried to go independent.

"Bought out? Yeah I suppose that's how they'd put it wouldn't they." They snorted, more amused than angry. "But yeah, that's where I was implanted. It means I run a little different than most." They smiled, letting him imagine just what they meant.

"Then they'd be lucky to work on someone as unique as you."

Chapter Nine

Eventually, the pair noticed everyone else had long since left, the small bar now cavernous in its quiet, broken only by Guin's intermittent bursts of laughter. It seemed Ryoma had a talent for making them smile. Autumn was milling around, tidying the bar, perhaps in the hope that the pair would take the hint and he wouldn't have to resort to shooing them away. The robovac was humming quietly as it tracked across the floor, sweeping away debris, cigarette ends, and spilled drink alike into its tank, politely slowing down as it approached the furniture.

As promised, Ryoma paid the drinks with his winnings and then some, feeling in his inebriated state, that an apology was in order for standing Autumn up on his last visit. He didn't go into detail why, but the bartender was more than forgiving when he saw the tip. "I've never seen River look that comfortable with anyone before, usually they've got one eye on the exit, you know?"

"Oh, uh, sure." He took the compliment, unsure what to make of it. They'd seemed nothing other than laid back since they met.

"You must be quite the charmer. Maybe I missed out the other night." He smiled, suggesting a far different evening that could have been.

"You hungry Ryo? I think I know a place nearby." Guin pressed against his back, their hand on his hip not going unnoticed. They inclined slightly and made for the exit, letting in the chill of evening air. "Thanks for staying open for us Aut."

With Guin leading the way, and Ryoma trying to keep up, they rounded the corner confidently proclaiming they knew the best route back to the main street, despite swaying on their feet slightly. Even with a synthetic body, alcohol could still work its magic. Ryoma followed closely behind them through a gloomy alley lit only by the eternal brightness of the main city without. Guin suddenly stumbled on an imperceivable imperfection on the ground, their silver shoes entangled. Ryoma darted forward to catch them, his heart racing when they clutched his arm in return, resting against the alley wall with a lazy smile.

"Hey, steady darling. I don't think I could fix you up as well as you looked after me."

The top buttons of their shirt had loosened throughout the night exposing the hollow of their throat, carrying the scent of their cologne, like spring rain. He remembered their voice from the night they'd met, murmuring softly as they repaired his arm, like spun gold.

"I'm sure you'd make a good doctor Ryo, you seem pretty interested in how I'm put together after all." Guin looked down into Ryoma's eyes, their gaze lingering on his lips just long enough for him to notice.

"You might have to teach me, but I'm a quick study."

"I'm sure you are." They grinned. "Why do you call me that? Darrrlin.'" Their voice slid down a couple of octaves as they elongated the word, settling comfortably into his accent. "You call everyone one that?"

He laughed at their pitch perfect impression. "Only if they're sweet, and ain't many as sweet as you. Just sounded right somehow. You don't mind, do you?"

"I like it, it's sort of old fashioned." They shrugged, affectionately stroking the stubble on his jaw. "No one's called me anything like that before."

Ryoma responded by pulling Guin closer, his synthetic hand on their slim waist, until he could feel the warmth in their core, their breath sweet from the drinks. For a second they did nothing, both unsure whether to make the first move, faces just barely apart and smiling uncontrollably. Just as the tension became unbearable Guin pressed their soft lips to his almost experimentally, then again, melting into him, the kiss deepening as both people realised just how hungry they were. Ryoma's hands quickly found their hips, untucking their shirt and pulling them closer, his lips burning, desperate for more.

"I haven't stopped thinking about you." He murmured when they finally broke apart, just enough to catch his breath. He gazed up at Guin; they stood a good few inches taller than him, looking beautifully elegant in the starlight that highlighted their sharp features, their aquiline nose. He tucked a loose strand of hair behind their ear and cupped the back of their neck guiding them down for another kiss, as sweet as their voice.

"I could tell, you've been looking at me with those big brown eyes all night, Ryo." Guin smiled, leaning back against the alley wall, and looking at him with animal hunger, like they'd swallow him whole. "You do this with everyone who picks you up off the street?"

"I try not to make a habit of it." It wasn't the worst way he'd hooked up with someone. In the distance he could hear groups of drunk tourists milling around, reminding them they weren't alone. "I'm staying in a room nearby, if you'd prefer some privacy."

Guin's eyes widened just a touch at the suggestion, leaving him wondering if he'd asked too soon. Their answer came when they took his hand with a coy smile. "Lead the way."

Ryoma fumbled with the keycard, missing a few times before the lock clicked open; Guin clung to his arm alternately giggling and murmuring about how much they wanted him. The pair fell into each other as it slid shut, just about making the few steps back onto the bed. The singer climbed on top of Ryoma, pushing him onto his back with barely a shove. They plucked open his shirt, pressing their lips to his neck, his chest, his-

"Ow shit," Ryoma hissed, clutching his side where a sharp pain dug into his ribs. He sat up gingerly on the edge of the bed, pulling his open shirt aside to take a look. Guin sat up straddling his waist, and touched the purple patch on his ribs, their fingers cooling his nerves. They seemed more curious than anything else. Never had to worry about this sort of injury, he thought, he must seem so delicate and fleshy by comparison. He laughed at the absurdity, at least until the contracted movement in his chest made him wince again. "You got me so worked up I almost forgot about all this."

"You're still so bruised up, did you go to a doctor?" They asked, still smiling but their voice was tinged with concern.

"It must have slipped my mind." Ryoma recovered his composure and shrugged out of his shirt, letting it drop to the floor. Between the case and the desire to see Guin again, he'd barely had a thought for taking care of himself. Not to mention the cost of seeing a real doctor. He leaned in again, pushing the ache to the back of his mind. "I'll be alright darling. Takes more than one bad night to break me."

"We'll just be careful." Guin still sounded apprehensive. "You can be on top if that's easier, I don't mind either way."

"No way, I like you right here." Ryoma grabbed their slender hips and held them in place, making a mental note of their versatility. He tilted their chin down, taking in those pretty green eyes. "You're not going anywhere, angel."

"If you insist." Guin shifted on his lap and threw their arms around his shoulders, getting comfortable. "I hoped you'd come back actually, after the other night. I'd hoped we could meet again."

"That so? Couldn't stop thinking about me?" A Cheshire grin erupted across his face, this wasn't doing his ego any favours.

Ryoma pulled them into a leisurely kiss, tucking a loose strand of hair behind their ear as he'd done before. He felt them shudder, just barely, as his fingers brushed the cool metal seam behind their ear.

"Does that feel good?"

"Yeah...those are a little sensitive, the contacts. Could you do that again?" They pressed their lips to his neck feverishly. "Please, Ryo. Please, touch me."

"Oh, well since you asked so politely." He stroked behind their ear, more purposefully this time. A low moan escaped their lips, the slight quiver in their voice left his jeans feeling tight. "You sing so well for me."

They cringed a little. "Sorry, I'm not usually like this."

"That's ok darling, make as much noise as you like." Ryoma hummed. "I want to hear you again."

He watched them shed their shirt, revealing the full extent of the ink he'd glimpsed earlier that night. Their slim chest was delicately inked with a writhing fish-snake creature, a mouthful of needle fangs bared. Its shimmering, ribbon-like, tail trailed down their stomach and disappeared under the waistband of their boxers. Exploring the length of the creature, he ran his hands over the ink, focusing downward and smoothly opening their belt to follow the tail as it trailed off below their belt. He slipped his hand into their waist band and found them already wet to the touch, yielding easily to his fingers.

"You're that worked up already?" He teased, bringing his fingers to his lips for a taste.

Sweet.

"So are you," they countered, giving him a gentle squeeze that made his breath hitch sharply. Their voice took on a playful edge that set his nerves on fire. "You were looking down my shirt all night, pervert."

"Then you better show me the rest, darling." The remainder of their suit bundled silently at the end of the bed, he hungrily watched the flickering lights cast from outside dance on their perfect body. The scent of their cologne had faded a little, down to a subtle base of vanilla and salt, filling his senses as they wrapped their arms around his shoulders.

They smiled softly, lips pink and parted at his attention, and pawed at his half opened jeans, making him shudder. "May I?"

He nodded breathlessly, his mouth kept occupied by theirs. A second later he felt their slick warmth press down on him, keeping a steady rhythm that made him light-headed. Their bodies fit together so well, they could have been made for him. He wanted to spend the night exploring all the ways he could make them tremble and cry out until they could take no more; though he suspected their stamina would outlast his. His hands wandered languidly over their back until he found the cool exposed metal in place of a spine, feeling each segment, each vertebrae flexing under his touch. Guin arched their back sharply and their eyes fluttered shut, body tensing around him.

They rode him harder, pulling a deep groan from his chest. "You're getting close, Ryo? You going to come for me?"

"Please, yes."

Ryoma smoked quietly from a stash he'd hidden from himself earlier that day and watched Guin doze in the darkened room, their clothes scattered across the snug little hotel room. The sheets were gathered at Guin's waist, seemingly immune to the chill of the air conditioning that had forced Ryoma to reach for his shirt. He was physically exhausted, but still couldn't sleep, with the light pouring in from the spaceport opposite the building and his mind consumed with the person next to him. Their soft expression briefly flickered with something akin to pain, and then quickly settled. A nightmare? He hoped he hadn't made a mistake; it didn't feel like a mistake.

He'd found himself with a lot of people over the years but it had never translated into anything lasting before. He'd just figured it wasn't for him, but looking at Guin, he was beginning to rethink that feeling. They'd seemed to fit together so well, intuiting each other's needs and wants easily, he'd never felt so compatible with someone before. Guin's tie lay crumpled on the bedside table under the low powered light, Ryoma let the texture of the satin weave between his fingers. He smirked, thinking how it had made for crude restraints, the both of them giggling, pretending the strength of their synthetic body couldn't easily shred it. Their body tensing and relaxing under him with each...

Guin jolted awake so suddenly that Ryo dropped his cigarette. He swore as he tried to grab it before it seared a hole in the sheets, pressing it between his lips for one more taste. Guin gazed up with a smirk, their eyes half lidded with sleep. "You'll lose your deposit, smoking in here like that."

"Think I already did. I'd say it was worth it though." He tilted his head toward the ceiling and exhaled, watching the smoke rise languidly until it caught the stream of the air processor. He crushed the remainder of his cigarette into the ashtray and summoned Guin closer with his free hand.

"You always pay your mechanics this way?" They shifted across the bed, resting their head on his chest. The sheet had fallen away but they didn't move to cover themself, and he wasn't complaining.

"Only when I'm short on credits, maintenance ain't cheap you know." He laughed and squeezed their bare hip.

"Have you been with someone like me before?"

Their question was vague, perhaps intentionally. "Usually I'm into guys, though I'm not tied to it. But a synth? You're my first." His hand slid between their legs, seeking the warmth between them. "How was I?"

"Huh, I wouldn't have guessed." Reaching up, their fingers softly brushed each of the freckles that speckled across his nose and cheeks. A mark of too much time under the twin suns. "I like these, they're very pretty."

"Pretty?" He laughed, flattered. No one had called him anything like that in a long time.

"You don't think so?" They cocked their head.

"It's just not a word I would use, darling." His silver hand traced along the frilled creature that coiled lazily across their torso. The ink had a shimmering opalescent quality, making the creature seem alive in the dimmed lights. "What's the story behind his ink? I've never seen anything glow like that before."

"It's just some basic bioluminescence, the ink glows by itself. Poisonous if you're organic, not so much for me." Their hand trailed down his arm, tracing the outline of his twin-tail. "It's a cliche, so many people from 'Phaestus have them in some form or another. You'll see a lot of them if you know people like me."

Now that he thought about it, the shape did look familiar. He'd seen the creature's head tattooed onto a few people, mostly synths. "I think I have, what is it?"

"They're thresher serpents. I mean, they're closer to fish than reptiles really, but the name stuck. They look like the monsters on those old maps, you know? Here be monsters." They sat up as they spoke, waving their hands expressively. "And huge too, must be about 100 feet some of them. They'd spawn in pools on the coast and they have these exposed spines kind of like I do. I always wondered if maybe they're all connected too, sharing everything."

They drew their fingers down their belly. He watched carefully as they touched where he had touched and kissed, the fire in his gut flickered. "They must be very special to you."

"Yeah, they are. Once they mature they disappear into the deep sea most of the time, and sometimes one would wash up, and they'd find it's a thousand years old. They're beautiful don't you think? I don't even know if there are any left now but..." They stammered, and stopped themself. "Sorry, I get carried away. It's easier to get across what I want to say when you're connected directly in the Hive, you know? You can just show people."

"Never connected to it but I've heard of it, yeah." They held his hand to their chest and Ryoma could swear he felt the gentle pulse there, making him wonder if their inner workings were not too different from his. "It's beautiful darling, you can tell me all you want. Are you thinking of getting more?"

"That's the plan, I think it needs a friend, don't you think? But I like to take my time working on the idea, I want to get it just right," Guin said, trying to contain a grin, he got the feeling not many people asked. "It's not like I'm limited on time, so..."

They trailed off, looking a little embarrassed, perhaps realising he didn't have the same experience. Guin leaned forward to look out of the window, the blinds were still half open, and the 'port was fully floodlit as always, it had kept Ryo awake most nights he'd been there. A combination of sleekly designed private and the more brutalist commercial craft thrummed as they took off in a chaotic buzz into the deep. "It's pretty isn't it?"

"The 'port?" He asked dubiously, it was just any other. Overpriced drinks and too busy for his liking. "It's nothing special."

"It's amazing we're out here really, that I can exist like this." They hugged their knees, the silver seam along their spine shining in the dimmed lights. Their hair fell forward, and Ryoma's attention was pulled to a spider-web of dark tissue at the base of their skull, textured where the synth-skin had tried to heal, but couldn't quite stitch itself together. It must have been a deep wound to scar like that, and a simple graft could hide it. Something about it felt familiar too, he had seen scars like that before, but he couldn't place where. Guin glanced back at him and his eyes snapped away, feeling ashamed at being caught. "There's some nice spots here and there, if you know where to look."

"So I've heard." He squeezed their shoulder, careful not to touch their neck. "Maybe next time you can show me."

"Next time?" They turned around, looking a little surprised, their face lit in lightly concealed enthusiasm.

"Well sure, if that's alright with you darling, I wouldn't mind seeing you play again." Not to mention that wickedly eager mouth of theirs.

"Sure, it's just... usually when people want to spend the night, they don't really come back. They're just passing through." Guin smiled softly, straddling his waist and playing with his fawny chest hair, squeezing the softened muscle on his belly, kissing his neck.

Who could ever leave someone like you?

"You're a sweet thing aren't you Ryo." He gave a wry smile as they lapped at his throat, groaning despite his exhaustion overriding any arousal.

"Oh fuck..."Gently he took hold of their wrist before they could tempt him further. "I don't think I can go again tonight, darling."

"Of course, sorry. It's just...you're really warm. It's nice." They murmured, relaxing into his arms, running their long fingers over a faded skin graft on his arm.

"I'm a little hot-blooded I guess." He reached for the blanket to pull over their shoulders. "You seem a little cold to me, if anything."

They chuckled softly, leaving him wondering what he'd said.

"Synthetic, remember? I don't have any blood at all." Ryoma chuckled, feeling a little stupid. Usually people complained that his synthetic arm was cold, the radiated heat from his body faded past the elbow. They caught each other's eye and kissed again, lips as soft as ever. "You'll really come back?"

He touched the cool seam behind their ear again, lips ghosting on theirs. "Of course."

Chapter Ten

Barely a week had passed when Ryoma had the itch to return. With no active cases, he found himself quickly bored but unwilling to take any new work after running himself into the ground so badly. His options seemed limited to milling around Polaris central with no purpose and money to burn, or to take himself offplanet and his thoughts quickly returned to the gilded nightclub filled with that husky sonorous voice. It didn't take much to convince him.

When he arrived, the 'port was in lockdown for over an hour, someone had tried to make off without paying their debts and casino security were tearing apart the place looking for them. When he finally arrived at the Reinhardt, slithering past security by wearing his old satin jacket and trying to style his hair into something appropriately 20th century, he caught Guin as they were just finishing their final set for the night. They spotted him lingering by the bar, eyes bright as they approached wordlessly. To make up for his lateness, he quickly bundled them into their compact dressing room, pushing the chair against the door.

"No interruptions this time."

"Eager aren't you?" They bit their lip, gripping the edge of the dressing table. They'd worn a little more makeup tonight, a few thin dark lines drawn from eyelid to temple, gold lip liner that framed their mouth as they spoke. He wished he'd seen them sing like this. Perhaps another night. "You've been thinking about this."

"Don't think I could stop if I tried."

"No?" They tugged at his shirt collar, mouth on his. "You sound like a man possessed."

"Said I'd come back, and I ain't one for lying if I can help it. How about I take you out proper? Seeing as I was late."

"How honourable of you." Their voice took on a mischievous tone, their delicate fingers tangling in his hair. "Although, I had something else in mind, if you want to show you're sorry..."

He felt them push very slightly and obediently he knelt between their thighs, pushing their skirt up. A few minutes later, a moan poured from their lips and he knew they were his.

It became their routine. His casino winnings, or rather, Guin's, would cover his trips for at least a little while. Even the noisy commercial ships back and forth didn't bother him so much, knowing who he'd see at the other end. They'd meet Ryoma at the door of the Reinhardt to allow him in, always dressed impeccably. Sometimes in their old fashioned suit, sometimes in a creamy purple dress the colour of the night sky, but always the same silver shoes that seemed to shimmer of their own volition. Guin would always offer to free up a booth for him to sit more comfortably, but he always refused. It became a little dance they did each time, a flirty back and forth. He wasn't there for luxury or comfort, he was there for them. He'd dress up as well as he could and watch them mystified every time, nursing a drink until their set was over.

Guin showed him some more of the quiet little bars tucked in the corners of the city, places where they could drink and talk. It seemed they'd picked up on his dislike of the crowded main city, even though he had never mentioned it, but he was glad they noticed. A few drinks in, they would head straight back to Guin's apartment, if they got that far. There were some snug little alleys on the way, and they'd frequently get sidetracked, fumbling like teenagers until a group of tourists or casino security forced them to move on.

Their modest living quarters were cramped and bare by any standard, but to Ryoma, it was a palace, even if most nights he was woken by the stray cat. She would scratch at the door in the early hours but Guin, who had taken to calling her Persimmon, happily got out of bed at any time to cater to her feeble meows, letting her settle on the end of the bed. They barely slept at all as far as he could tell, he only caught them if he got up in the night, his own scattershot sleeping pattern made more than a few hours at a time difficult. When Guin woke, they always woke abruptly, body tense and eyes wide with the panic of being yanked from a nightmare, something he was closely accustomed to. They never spoke when this happened, they just pressed themself against him, head resting on his chest until they drifted back to sleep. He didn't ask, the scar on their neck told him enough.

A few weeks passed, and one morning Ryoma woke to the local star gloomily breaking through the blinds, light landing on the already busy Guin. The sheets gathered at their hips as they perused through a small stack of music notation, humming the notes to themself.

They smiled without looking up. "Morning Ryo, if you can call it that. Didn't need to be anywhere urgent, did you?"

He groaned and checked the scratched up display on his wrist. "Shit, I didn't mean to sleep that long. I can head out if you want, don't want to get in your way, darling."

The truth was, he did have some work to do. There were a couple of background checks in his inbox that still needed attention. Simple work really, an afternoon at most but his motivation was low especially when he could be here instead. Even after a month of this, part of him still expected Guin to get sick of him. There was still time for them to realise he was no good.

Guin leaned over and pressed their lips to his. "There's no rush, I'm not singing again until tomorrow night. How about coffee?"

"Please." Maybe a little longer wouldn't hurt.

Slipping their music under the bed, they picked up his creased maroon shirt from last night, and threw it over their shoulders. They were far too tall and the shirt was much too short to cover much of anything. Hungrily, he watched them leave, thinking about the soft curve of their thighs wrapped around his waist, until the cat jumped into his field of view, demanding his full attention. Perci stood in the residual warmth of the bed and began to knead the sheets with determined claws. Ryoma tentatively stroked her chin as he'd seen Guin do and listened to the low roll of her purrs, layered over the soft clattering of activity in the kitchen.

"I see you're a fan too, huh? Cute aren't they?" He smiled.

The cat squeaked a response and curled into a ball to settle in for a nap. He sat lost in thought, feeling her short coarse fur between his fingers until he heard the clinking porcelain close by. Guin standing in the doorway with a faint smile, watching their modest collection of waifs and strays gathered on the bed. They passed him a cup, which he took gratefully, and sat next to him carefully to avoid waking the cat, and crossed their long legs in an attempt at modesty. "Perci really likes you. She looks for you when you're not here. Usually she doesn't like strangers so much."

"That so? I'll have to stay more often, won't I?" He took a sip of his drink, the taste lingering on his tongue. The fragrant raspberry and pluot notes of the coffee began to wake him up through just aroma alone, better than the hollow nervous energy from a stim.

Maybe it was the way they made it, or maybe it was just sharing it with them, but it made him feel like he could stay here forever. Living together in this cosy little apartment, they would sing and he'd pick up whatever work he could. Carve out a life, just the two of them. "A guy could really get used to this."

"My room is always open to you Ryo. If you'll have it."

"Thank you, Guin. You know, I've been wanting to ask, is that your given name or River, or ..."

"It's just, Guin. I started going by River when I came here, it was an impulse really, I wanted a fresh start and it sort of stuck with the people around here. Well, the ones who even know my name at least. People come and go a lot around here." They paused for a sip, eyeing him carefully. "You must be the only person here who knows my true name."

"Really? I'm honoured." Emotion swelled in his chest.

"You trusted me to take care of you that night, so I trust you to know me. I had a different name when I was very young, before all this." They gestured loosely at their body. "But it didn't really feel like me. A lot of things didn't."

It seemed like the more time they spent together, the more they had in common, despite how different they had appeared. He hadn't even considered their life before, that they'd once had an organic body. "I know that feeling, Ryoma weren't always my name neither. It's been so long I can hardly remember what it was before."

"Me either. But I like Ryoma. I think it suits you." They leaned over, cradling their cup in one hand so as not to spill it and pressed their lips to his, their commandeered shirt left invitingly open.

"It was strange, when I heard it for the first time, it just felt like it was always my name."

"That's what it's like when it rings true. Perhaps you were always Ryoma, you just needed to remember."

"Yeah. I guess when you know, you know." He watched them fuss over the cat, letting her tail snake between their long fingers and he was struck by the feeling that he could really fall for them. Years from now they could be doing this, coffee and breakfast. Performing light maintenance on each other as they grew older. But would Guin grow older? Would they still want him when he was hundred and they looked the same? Words caught in his throat.

"What's going on up there, Ryo?" A hand touched his bare shoulder.

You're getting too close, too soon.

"How, how long have you been around? The way you talk sometimes, you've been alive since Polaris was founded at least. If you don't mind me asking."

"It's alright with me, I don't get that many people asking. Uh let me see..." They stared off for a second, trying to recall it from their long term memory. "I must be up to decade sixteen-ish by now, it gets hard to keep track of individual years after a while. Maybe in the low one-seventies."

They blinked as the data retrieval completed, that synth-assisted memory must come in handy. "Ah here we go, one hundred and sixty two, by standard time if that matters, and a hundred days, so not a bad guess. My internal clock can't be that far off."

"One-sixty?" He laughed, trying to process how much time that was, Polaris would have been a barely terraformed mining platform back then. His ancestors would have been considering leaving the increasingly isolationist Mars. "You don't look a single day over a hundred, if I do say so."

"You're very sweet."

"I suppose this makes me your sugar baby don't it. It's my birthday soon you know. Big four oh." That must be nothing to them, he thought, a blink of the eye. A hundred years from now would they even remember him?

"I'll have to get you something special, I never even notice mine passing." They shrugged and took a sip. "Maybe there's something about being long lived, time becomes this liquid thing after a while. Things seem to go past very quickly and slowly at once, so it stops making sense to even keep count really."

"I can't imagine, we must seem like mayflies to you."

They cringed, embarrassed. "I've offended you, I'm sorry. I forget that people can find that weird to hear about, if they're not the same."

"I asked, didn't I? It ain't weird, it's just different. I like different." He shuffled along to bed towards them.

"I suppose I am a little unusual, especially around here."

"You don't see too many synths moonlighting as jazz singers, or at all for that matter. Especially not here." He remembered the house rules at the casino he'd wandered into, made sense they would avoid the main strip, not much point going somewhere you're not wanted.

"No I suppose you don't, when 'Phaestus was dissolved, nearly everyone left rather than work under new management, not after they wrecked the ocean anyway. That was the best thing about that place. there's not much left of what was."

"Sounds familiar."

"A lot of us migrated inward and disappeared into the other colonies, some even had their contact seams sealed up so people couldn't tell what they were. Became mech-medics or navigators. Things were pretty messy back then. They still are, I suppose."

"Not sure things have ever been calm, least not in my lifetime." He knew that ache that came with losing your home, even if it was a crappy mining rock in the first place. "Where did you go, if you don't mind me asking? You got a new home?"

"I went with some others to start again elsewhere, Polaris actually. But after what happened..."

"Nothing feels stable does it."

"I was so afraid it'd all fall apart again. I just left, rather than go through it all again. Left everyone I knew, family even. I haven't seen my brother in so long." Their expression shifted, their airy smile crumbling under the weight of memory. They'd never mentioned family before.

"And well, to cut a few years of wandering short, I sort of washed up here a while ago, and I took a liking to the place. I always liked to sing, and they gave me a chance at the Reinhardt even though I barely knew anything about the place. I always thought of going back or even just contacting the other synths, but I couldn't bring myself to."

They shrugged; their energy seemed to have drained away suddenly. Ryoma was curious but knew he had no right to pry, that was just the investigator in him poking around. He barely knew anything about synth subculture aside from what tidbits Sylph had mentioned over the years, and those he'd met previously were reluctant to tell an outsider.

"Hephestus was a little before my time. Synthetics built by synthetics right? That's all I remember people telling me about it."

"That was the idea, a brave new world. So much for that." They laughed softly at his naivety, which he hoped meant they found it amusing rather than ignorant.

"Sounds like a dream."

"Yeah, it was. We just wanted to get out from under the thumb of the corps. They charge what they like and you can't refuse when it's what keeps you alive. I'm sure you've felt the sting of that." They looked at his arm, then bit their lip, stopping themself.

"It's ok, you're right. Just having my arm looked at ain't cheap, I can't imagine what it costs for you. Are you Hephestus-made?"

They shook their head. "Not originally. I'm an old BioMech model; the Venus something or other. But when we went independent, I had a full refurb, much more complex than what they could make. Insides stripped down to the brainwork. They couldn't extract all the 'mech junk without brain damage so there'll always be a little bit of them left, but most refits are like that."

"So you might say you've voided your warranty." He took a long languid look at them, stretched out on the bed, their shirt barely clinging on.

"Oh sure!" They laughed, their mood lifted. "A dozen times over, I don't think any licensed mechanic in the outer systems would even recognise what I've got going on inside, except maybe a few grey market guys who've dealt with smuggled parts. But I'd say your arm isn't factory fresh either."

"I've had a little bit of work done on the side." A few hasty adjustments between fights to keep him going an extra round, on top of the engraving work, meant his mechanic always found a way to add something to the bill, complaining about how it damaged the structural integrity of the piece. Who'd have thought a few thin lines carved into the surface would cause so much trouble. He knew it was bullshit, but paid all the same.

"I wouldn't say that too loud, you'll get it repossessed for that." They giggled, only half joking. "A synth mechanic - a real one, not some amateur like me, would be able to keep that running forever."

"I'd love that. Never worrying about this damn thing. Always wanted to visit Hephaestus, seems a shame BioMech chewed it up like they did." He said distantly. "Same thing happened where I grew up, they cracked it open for the core."

"It's parasitic what they do."

They sat in silence for a moment, remembering their respective lost homes.

"You uh, you could all connect together right? I've got a synth friend who keeps trying to tell me but I can't make heads or tails of it."

"With the synapse pools? Yeah sure, if you've got one you can hook into the hive. Anyone can really, but these things here give you a stronger connection, help you process it easier." They tapped behind the shell of their ear. "You feel a lot more too. Some people spend all their time in synapse-gel, you can even get lost if you're under for too long, swim a little too deep. Then on the other side of it, some people bounce right off, totally hate the feeling, it's a very personal thing really."

"What's it like, in there?"

"In the hive? It's..." They sat up and thought for a second, grasping for a means to verbalise. "When you're in the pools, and you're linked in, it's like you're diving but there's no sea floor, and you never need to surface. So you just keep going and going, and it's endless, it's like a dream, and it always remembers you. It feels like home." They gazed serenely into their coffee. "Have you tried connecting before?"

"I haven't, I just thought it was some kind of VR." He'd only seen it as an expensive gimmick experience in vacation retreats, sold as some wish fulfilment exercise. His sister had tried to drag him along once on Polaris but he'd made his excuses. The idea of being in a tank alone with his thoughts had little appeal to him.

"It's so much more than that, it's, it's hard to explain, really. You feel like a little fish swimming around a coral reef, looking for others like you, making your own little space." They climbed onto his lap, their infectious excitement pulling him along for the ride. "I'd love to show you one day, there's still a few pools around if you know where to look. The connection is less intense outside the original pools on Hephaestus but once you're submerged, it's like we never left. I could take you for a dip."

"It sounds beautiful. I don't see why'd you'd ever leave."

"The isolation can be calming but..." Their hand softly brushed his. "After a while you start to crave something physical, or I do at least. I like being somewhere more populated, more real to be a little crude. Despite the risks, I could never live in there, like some do." Their hand drifted to the back of their neck, seemingly without realising.

He glanced around at the rundown interior, the obtrusive neon lights from the bar next door crept through the curtain and threw a pallid green glow over the room. "There's got to be better places than this, less separated from your people."

"For sure, there are synth collectives tucked away if you know where to look, but there's a charm to this place. The casino is a scam but everyone knows it, the drinks are too expensive, and everything's just a little gaudy, on the very edge of taste. Very Late Terran, don't you think?"

"I'll take your word for it." He had no idea about Terra, but he loved hearing them talk. They made it sound like a fantasy, a dream to be here. But looking at them, there was a sadness in their eyes that betrayed something else.

"It's an interest of mine, Terran history and music, it's a little silly I suppose. Unlike what you do, I'm sure that's much more important. What kind of cases do you take? Anything exciting?"

Ryoma shrugged, he'd tried to keep them separate from his work as much as he could, his stay with Guin was supposed to be a respite from all that. Even so, he couldn't help but notice a steady flow of messages from Sylph over the last week, but he'd been too distracted to listen to them. Perhaps she'd found something on the Rearden case, part of him hoped not for fear it would burst the bubble of his newly found calm. "Oh, all sorts, mainly just tracking wayward spouses, background checks on spouses and business partners."

"Do you look for missing people?" An oddly specific question.

"Uh, sure. Most of the time it's people getting hooked on those VR suites like Wonderland and forget about the outside 'till you wake them up. They ain't too happy when I'm the first real thing they see in six months, I can tell you. Sometimes it's someone with half a head of brainwork got 'jacked, and you find them ditched halfway across the system once the creeps have had their fun."

He noticed their body visibly stiffen at the mention of jacking, their hands gripping the mug for comfort. Too late he realised why he'd seen the scarring on their neck before. A puncture like that was a quick and dirty way to get into the nervous system. Left a hell of a nasty scar but not every 'jacker cared about hiding their attack. He cleared his throat and tried to mitigate. "But you know, it's mostly screen work though, scanning through hours of surveillance, security records, digging through trash, that sort of thing. It ain't that sexy really."

"You're being modest," Guin said, shoulders loosening. "Sounds like you're pretty good at what you do. Nice to know that if I vanished someone like you would look for me."

"I'd try my best darling."Ryoma felt a pang of guilt for ignoring his work for so long, his unanswered ear bud on the bedside table. "Do you disappear often?"

They looked up at him with an unreadable expression. "I've been known to."

Chapter Eleven

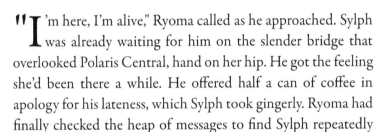

"**I**'m here, I'm alive," Ryoma called as he approached. Sylph was already waiting for him on the slender bridge that overlooked Polaris Central, hand on her hip. He got the feeling she'd been there a while. He offered half a can of coffee in apology for his lateness, which Sylph took gingerly. Ryoma had finally checked the heap of messages to find Sylph repeatedly requesting they meet urgently with varying degrees of terseness. After a phone call of largely grovelling apologies they'd organised to meet as soon as he arrived back on world.

"Good to know," she said, surveying the man in front of her, he looked surprisingly well put together for someone off the back of a day's worth of travel. "You look a lot better than the last time I saw you."

"Yeah well, the medicine on Scylla ain't half bad." He remembered a cool hand on his shoulder.

"So it would seem." Sylph turned and headed further into the city. "Do you mind if we walk and talk? Surveillance and all. I'm staying just inside the under-city. You remember Simul, right?"

"Uh sure." He let her lead, even though he knew the way. As a boxer he'd fought there semi-regularly, the underground fights were illegal but the cut was better than commercial, which was what counted when you needed to make rent. There was a pause as the pair shared the rest between them, the can running dry. Crumpling it flat, Ryoma tossed the remaining disc into a clunking recycler as they passed, the bot bleeping in acknowledgement. The street suddenly became dark where the buildings overhead had become merged with a bridge to link them, and the city suddenly felt more private and comfortable. The tension that gripped his shoulders in the exposed upper-city, relaxed.

They came to one of the many pre-fab tower blocks in the district where Sylph slid a faded keycard through a scanner. The entrance to Simul slid open, revealing a tight dimly lit corridor with heavy self locking doors either side. She led him halfway down and tapped in a code faster than he could process. To call it a living space seemed like a misnomer, occupied by computing equipment stacked waist high, a desk and screen he recognised from his call with her a few weeks past.

"You're staying here? Thought you were moving on soon."

"Temporarily. It's secure at least, no ID checks. Here, look at this." Sylph produced a flexible transparency seemingly from thin air, one of her party tricks, and with a flick of her wrist it became opaque, the text now readable against the cluttered desk.

"This is what I've got so far." She scrolled through a tangled web of registered corporate entities, some owned by others further up the chain, others separate but operating in the same market. "It's a mess as you can see. That's why it took me so long to find you anything worth reporting."

He looked at the lists of names, none of which seemed familiar to his eye at least. Half were probably shells. "What does that mean?"

"Means whoever he's working for is putting a lot of effort into obscuring what they're doing. Could just be the usual secrecy in development, I mean he works for a synthetics developer..."

"But you don't think so?" She wouldn't have kept looking if that was the case.

"This doesn't feel like that, I think your gut was right on this one."

"Ah, shit. I was hoping this would be easy, I hate all this hacker crap."

"That's what you get for being curious. This was barely hacking by the way, these guys need to work on their security."

"Maybe you should do it," he said dryly.

"Couldn't pay me anything to do that, leeches. Rearden's employer is based here, got a public facing outlet in Central. It's registered as a brainwork developer with a showroom, quite popular around here with the upper-city sorts too."

"Raxle Specialist Engineering," he read. "Never heard of them."

"You wouldn't have, well out of your price range."

"That bad?"

She snorted. "Grotesque. Their listings say something about proprietary brainwork synapsing, nothing on the net so they must keep it heavily guarded. Might still be in the testing phase."

Usually that was the aim for companies starting out in this system, hoping the scouts for BioMech or Nacht would notice and secure a decent pay day and settle. But it was a fine line to walk, create anything too threatening to either corp and you didn't last too long. The hostile takeover of Hephaestus had sent a message; don't get too bold, or we'll take what you have.

"Did you find anything on the woman?"

Sylph shook her head. "Absolutely nothing, she's a ghost. Lends credence to your conspiracy theory. She could be his corp handler, or worse."

He shivered, an encounter with an enforcer would be a death sentence.

"Those guys that beat you up on the other hand were just common or garden heavies. Each one had a list of clients as long as my arm."

"Just another job."

"Maybe between getting into street brawls you can check this showroom out." She slapped him on the back.

"I think I'll find time." He looked at the name on her tab, committing it to memory. "Raxle Specialist Engineering, I'll take a look."

"And I'll keep my ear to the ground with the 'hacker crap', see if I can't find where that data stick went after you saw it." She took on an ersatz offended tone. "It's hard for anyone to go silent running, unless they know what they're doing. You know, I didn't think this would be your sort of case, no offence."

She was right, he'd always preferred to lean into the simple cases, easy pay days kept a roof over his head.

"Not intentionally, those were always Serena's deal, she wanted the big scores, she wanted to help people," Ryoma said, surprising himself. He'd never made a habit of mentioning her unprompted. "I was just there to growl at people, throw a punch or two if things got out of hand."

"You're more than that. She'd be proud of you, her little brother keeping the business going."

"Little? We were twins."

"She told me she was born first." She shrugged. "That makes you the little brother, far as I can tell."

"Of course she told you that, that's just like her," he scoffed.

"You're actually in a good mood for once." She noted with a smile. "Did I miss something the last few weeks?"

"I'm always in a good mood, you've just not seen me in a while."

"Not from what I remember Ryo, you're a miserable bastard if I recall rightly." She cackled at his scowl. "I think you got a little more than medicine on your work trip, huh? Who is he?"

"Sylph..." She had this way of weedling things out of him, not unlike his sister. "They, actually. It's very new, we're just seeing how it goes." He was much more far gone than that, he just hoped Guin felt the same.

"Huh, well, I'm glad you're keeping yourself busy with something other than work." She eyed him carefully. "That's a good thing, Ryo."

"Nice to know someone's keeping track."

"Say, if I continue to help you, can I meet your mystery friend? I want to know who's responsible for making you smile like that."

"It's early days yet, but I'll consider it," he said, unsure how he'd propose that to Guin. From what he'd manage to skim, they hadn't left Scylla in a few years at least. Probably more considering their perception of time.

"Of course, I'd hate to be sprung on anyone, not too many full synths around, I might scare them away."

"I don't think that'll be a problem, in the meantime I'll give this showroom a look, after breakfast. Had to run here from the 'port."

"I could tell

The Raxle showroom was situated in the dead centre of the upper-city, occupying the ground floor of an obscenely tall spire. Ryoma tidied himself up the best he could in the hope of passing as someone used to having a few credits in hand. For a tech start-up, their backers must have deep pockets, the building was far too luxurious, unnaturally clean and bright, definitely someone with money to burn. Inside, there were a few other customers following consultants around and discussing options.

Next to him a wall flickered to life, and a smooth computerised voice ran through an extensive greeting and a gushing spiel, listing off the company's achievements in 'just a few short years.' Ryoma's contact lens picked up on the sensor embedded in the screen, scanning his face for this ID, any unlicensed implants, and most importantly the credits in his account. He'd had more than a few doors slam shut in his face for being flat broke before, but for once he actually had the money to show for it. Still, he felt like he was going to get caught out. Finally, it gave him an opening. "How can we help you?"

"I'm looking to talk to someone about a brainwork upgrade, and I heard you were the best. Any chance I could get a demo?"

"We are extremely busy at this time, please accept our apologies as we would hope to provide the best service possible. Please proceed to the waiting area whilst a consultant becomes available for you, sir." Ryoma sat in the clinically decorated reception, the chairs injection moulded into a glossy single piece of plastic. He fidgeted in the uncomfortable and clammy seat, idly clenching his right fist where it ached. The weather would probably change soon, it was the end of the summer. Through the filtered window, he could see the sparsely populated street, corp enforcers moving people along if they looked like they'd come from the Under.

Ryoma had been here a handful of times over the years, usually when trying to impress dates or when a date was trying to impress him, but now he lacked the desire, and often the credits, to bribe his way into any of the decent bars. Despite being inside and assumed to be a paying customer, he sank in his seat out of habit; he was an interloper here.

"Mr, uh, LeBeau?" He looked up at a face he'd only seen from afar before. Dayne Rearden was taller up close.

"That's me." This was certainly unexpected, no doubt it was Sylph's way of helping.

"I'm Dr. Rearden, I'm afraid there's no consultants at the moment as you can see so I'll have to do. If you'll come with me?" He seemed more at ease than he had on Scylla, the Doctor title was bunk though. Ryoma was led through to a bright office, the back wall lined with a few generations of synthetic brainwork overlaid onto ceramic skulls, spanning from the external memory aids to paper thin implanted hardware. The man looked at Ryoma as he sat behind the desk. "Sorry to ask but, have we met?"

Shit.

"I don't think so, not unless you spend a lot of time in the Under." He didn't bother suppressing his accent this time.

"Oh, sorry, you just seem familiar." This nose wrinkled just a touch. No of course, you wouldn't know anyone from *there*. Still, he couldn't help but notice the telltale indents on the man's wrists, haptic connectors from cheap VR suites could leave a bruise if you were a frequent flyer. You didn't get those up here.

"Must have one of those faces."

"Yes, my mistake." He tugged at his sleeves. "So how can I help?"

"I'm interested in some brainwork, my memory's not what it used to be." He blinked a couple of times to record, wandering over to the skeletal busts along the wall in feigned interest. We wondered if Guin had something like this. "I had a little luck in Scylla and was hoping to make a good investment, and that's what you're meant to do, right? Someone told me you're the best around."

"That's incredibly lucky, sir. I've never been myself, I'm somewhat married to my work." Even he sounded unconvinced by his lie and quickly trailed off before he could elaborate further, changing the subject. The two of them discussed specs, Ryoma working from the loose memory of what Serena had installed. That had been over a decade ago, but it meant Dayne was able to talk more and Ryo could sit back and get a better read on him, close up. His eyes were bruised too, pale enough to look like he hadn't slept to most but Ryoma knew better. Reality was too much for some.

"Well I can tell you we're working on some interesting things right now, we've received some new investment recently and it's allowed us to work on the next generation of synthetics." He became far more animated as he spoke, it was the nervous energy of someone talking about a specific interest of theirs.

"Anyone I'd know about?" Ryoma tried his best to sound interested. Considering the market, it could really only be one of the two manufacturers even if it was a subsidiary funding them.

"You'll, you'll have to excuse me, I really shouldn't say." He reeled back in, but he'd already said too much. He sniffed a sale, and it was making him sloppy.

"I understand, industry secrets and all. So what makes this better?"

"A full brain overlay, instant memory back-up, negligible data degradation, potentially unlimited life span, with regular maintenance of course."

"Of course. What are we talking about here, I'd be like those full bodies?"

Rearden looked nervous suddenly, he'd clearly said more than he was meant to, eager to impress. "Well sir, we can't say for sure, but we're about to start human trials, and results so far have been extremely promising. Perhaps we can get you on the waiting list for when they go to market, if you're interested?

"How much is this gonna cost me?" He tried to sound curious rather than cheap.

"Well, who can put a price on such things?"

You guys do.

"I think I'd want to see something concrete before I put anything down."

"Of course." He swivelled the screen on his desk, jostling a couple of loose tokens on his desk. Ryoma recognized them from one of the seedier VR-cades he'd fished a few people from in his time. "If you'll look here you can see the brain work integration from the current and the prototype."

"I see." He leaned in for a closer look, hoping the cheap replacement contact would hold up. The resolution would be poor and the text grainy, it wasn't really meant for anything other than identifying people, but it was better than nothing. Looking at the display he had little to no idea what anything meant, aside from it was meant to demonstrate their products' superiority. Perhaps it was another project for Sylph to review when he saw her next, adding it to the rapidly accumulating stack of favours he owed. "I think I'll need some time to think about all this." Rearden didn't seem to hear, his eyes had glazed over staring into nothing across the room.

"Oh, uh. Of course, sir." He fiddled with the understated wedding band on his finger. "You'll have to excuse me, my uh, I haven't been myself recently, I lost someone very dear to me recently."

A loss? Maybe he was lying, but what reason would he have to?

"Transport accident... you think they'd be safer you know?" His voice was distant, stilted.

Ryoma shifted uncomfortably on the spot, he had to get out of here, now.. "Shit, you know I just remembered. I have an appointment this afternoon to get to, I'll be in touch."

The man nodded distantly as he made a beeline for the exit.

Ryoma's heart pounded, he tugged the top button of his shirt loose to stop from feeling like he was choking, trying not to break into a run. He'd done it again, he'd got someone killed. Rounding the corner from the glossy office building, he threw up in an alley, his breakfast splattering onto the floor.

"Hey...! Too much to drink buddy?" A group of tourists jeered nearby, clearly enjoying their first trip to Central.

"Eat shit." He growled, shuddering.

Chapter Twelve

A broken night's sleep followed, Ryoma sporadically dreaming of a deep nothingness that tore at him, pulling him away from his sister, his friends, Guin, until he snapped awake, feeling like he'd been hollowed out. Craving the fresh air, he jimmied open the stiff window and took a shaky breath, the sounds of the city below breaking the suffocating silence of the apartment. Ryoma's nightmares fell away as the chill morning air flowed inward until he shivered, and tried to focus on the myriad noise of conversations and machinery below.

Still here, I'm still here.

Slowly, his stomach settled, and reason returned to him. He crawled out of bed and flicked on his tab, greeted with the results of his haphazard research from the night before. With a little digging he'd found a reference to her on the feed. Elise Rearden was dead. Engine failure, one of a thousand things that could go wrong. Or be sabotaged. She'd been Terran, born to impossible wealth as he'd imagined, although she was disinherited for leaving. Perhaps she'd meant to make amends with her impending divorce. Now he'd never know. He barely knew anything about her and here he was getting her killed.

Next to him, his ear bud softly bleeped on the table. He could have sworn he'd switched it off. Sighing he picked it up, hoping to get rid of whoever it was.

"Ryo?" The chatter in the background was so noisy it was hard to make out Guin's voice. But it was them sure enough.

"Guin?"

"I took your number from your card, I hope you don't mind. I'm at the 'port in Central, figured I'd come to you this time, since it's your birthday."

He checked the date on his wrist. The scuffed face still needed replacing.

"So it is." He'd forgotten entirely, having spent the last couple largely drunk and losing the subsequent days to the lingering threads of a hangover.

"You mentioned it once and I thought I'd surprise you, Aut's looking after Perci for me. Besides, you've come all the way to the Scylla, stayed all that time. I should come to you at least once. Although I'm, uh, afraid I don't know the area that well, it's been a few decades since I was here. Wasn't quite as built up before. I'm by a statue of, huh, you know I have no idea what this thing is meant to be."

Recognizing their confusion, he knew exactly where they were. "The Chipset? Yeah, stay put I'll come get you." He made a dash for the shower and shoved on a fresh set of clothes, dissolving a stim under his tongue for a boost before leaving.

Across the city, he found Guin perched on the edge of the low plinth below the warped sculpture; they'd taken his request not to move rather literally.

"Weren't waiting long were you?" He asked, trying not to sound too winded. They watched him huff, amused that he'd clearly run at least part of the way. It was unusual to see them out of their usual formal wear, a simple dark coloured jumpsuit, the zipper left open enough for the top of their tattoo to show. Their serpentine guardian.

"Not long. It was nice to wait, I did a little people watching," they said, turning to read the plate next to the statue. " 'To commemorate the bicentennial of the founding, in grateful collaboration with BioMechanics.' They really do get everywhere don't they?"

"Hm. The local government delegated day to day control of Polaris a while back, the thing you're sitting on is supposed to represent the synergy between people and business, I think."

"Sounds like them. There was rumour they wanted to buy out Scylla, but the owners wouldn't budge, didn't want to lose independence I suppose."

"Those casinos must rake in the credits I reckon."

"Enough to give them some leverage. Anyway, what would you like to do? Your day after all." They produced a small package beside them. "And I got you this, it's not much. I've never really celebrated mine so I'm not sure what you're supposed to get people."

He took the neatly wrapped box. "You shouldn't have."

"Oh. Should I not?" They straightened up, nervously eyeing the box.

"No, I mean. Thank you, Guin." He squeezed their shoulder and pointed down the street with his chin. "Come on, I'll show you where I'm at." They held out their hand loosely and let him lead them further into the metropolis, weaving through the crowds and abruptly landing taxis through to the

Under. The static clean of the corp maintained area gave way to the self-run part of the city, the patchworked air processors clinging to the sides of buildings.

"You said you'd been here before?"

"A long time ago. This was the main city back then, and that chrome tangle back there was just a simple 'port. Couple of ships a day at most."

"Huh." Must have been long before his time. "You said you've never had a birthday?"

"I mean, I think I did when I was really young but not in recent memory, I think it's less of a novelty, the longer you're around."

"Suppose it ain't that special when you're not on the clock," he thought out loud.

"Maybe we can try next time mine comes around. Although I guess there could be a couple of dates if you include when I was implanted," they wondered aloud.

They drifted away from him and looked up at the towering buildings that reached out into the deep, the sky tinged with orange light pollution. It seemed there was no true darkness anywhere. Ryoma watched Guin for a moment as they came to a stop, taking in their surroundings, they seemed so small. People parted to give them a wide berth, the shimmer of the contacts behind their ears were attracting glances, a few stares too.

"Guin!" He called them over. "Are you alright?"

"Yeah I am. It's just that..." Their voice was strained with uncertainty, lost in a maze that was so familiar to him. "I don't remember any of this. I thought I would see something, feel something once I was here, but it's all so different now."

"It's changed a lot down here, even since I arrived." He pressed his wrist to the door until it clicked open. "Here, I'm in this building. It's a little quieter up there. Maybe we can find something you recognize."

Guin followed a few paces behind, ducking their head under the door frame as they joined him. They gazed out of the elevator window at the city watching the flow of traffic as cars and taxis negotiated the airspace, not without a little passive aggressive honking. As the elevator slowed a twin-tailed lizard skittered up the drainpipe next to them, its ridged feet gripping on despite the pull of gravity half a mile up.

"Tough aren't they?" They watched, entranced by the creature. With their hair tied back, he could see the top of the raised scarring above their collar.

"Yeah, they are." He touched their slim wrist as the elevator slowed to a stop. "We're here."

Guin wandered the narrow perimeter of his apartment, fascinated with every small detail, running their hand along the edges of the furniture they passed. It was rare for him to have visitors during the day, and his hodge podge of furniture he'd rescued from the office was probably unusual to the eye.

"It was nicer when I moved in a few years back, I'm not much of a housekeeper." He watched them look around the room, resisting the urge to attempt to tidy whilst they were occupied. If they noticed coffee rings on the table, the laundry mountain, the beer cans, they didn't say. Perhaps they'd seen worse. "It's close to central back there, which is where all the well-paying clients come from, so it's a good place to be. The landlord's some programme that shifts the rent up every year or so. If you don't pay, your keycard just stops working. I've managed to keep pace so far, but who knows."

"That's awful, it's...inhuman."

"Yeah but, world keeps turning all the same. Ain't much we can do about it." They didn't look convinced, and he could feel they didn't agree. Changing the subject, he tapped the box they'd given him. "So what's this little thing?"

"I'm not telling." Guin shook their head. "I know I said I don't know much about birthdays, but I think you're meant to open it."

He held up the gift, examining the slightly haphazard wrapping with a grin. The longer he knew them, the more the little gaps in Guin's knowledge became visible. They'd go a little blank around some social normalcy he'd never think of, it was cute.

"Huh, is that so? Let's see shall we." With some careful unwrapping, he looked inside and slid open the top of a small circular silver case. Inside was a brand new communications contact, far better than his old one, sitting in its dock. He balanced it carefully on the tip of his finger trying to see the circuitry in the suns-light.

"It's shatterproof, and gloss coated to replicate the eyeball, so it shouldn't be visible at all to most people. I was thinking it would be less likely to get stolen. Is it ok?" Their voice was a little hopeful, a little anxious.

"That's so sweet darling. But this thing's far too expensive for me."

"It's nothing Ryo, really. I told you, I never know what to do with money. I don't eat much, I don't need anything really, and I thought it would make you happy. Figured I'd put what I've got to some use."

"I'll give it a try when I'm working, angel." He tucked back a loose lock of their hair. "Thank you." They leaned down for a kiss, pulling him closer with a gentle tug on the thin chain around his neck, their mouth soft and pliable to the touch.

"How about you give me a tour?"

He glanced around the compact living room and kitchenette, it was bigger than Guin's place but only just. It didn't help that he wasn't much of a homemaker. "Ain't much to show, just this and the bedroom."

"Well, maybe you could show me that, I've wondered about you." They hummed, playing with his shirt buttons. "You can be so quiet about yourself."

"There's not much mystery to me." There had to be a hundred washed up guys like him in this building alone, he thought. But only one of them.

"That contact has a record function you know, could be fun."

Ryoma grinned wolfishly, the easy-open jump suit they wore began to make sense. "Well of course darling, we better make sure this little thing works."

He pinched the zipper between thumb and finger and lowered it to their stomach, the cool green glow on their chest inviting him in. They slid it the rest of the way down to their waist and pushed the garment from their shoulders to the floor, fabric gathering at their ankles. Nothing beneath. "Perfect."

He took their wrist, pocketing their gift, and led Guin through to the bedroom...

Afterward, he collapsed back on the bed, his whole body feeling so light he could have floated away.

"We can watch that back later, if you like." Guin peered out of the window at the city below them. They still sounded so energised, ready for another round already.

"Sure I think I'll need a break though, some of us are fleshy and tired, and old."

"You don't seem to mind so much, letting me wear you out." They pressed their ear to his chest, as they always did, and tangled their long legs with his. Their hair tie disappeared during their dalliances, letting their hair fall loose.

"You're listening to me aren't you? To my heart." He wondered how many heartbeats he had left in him, how many breaths. Could they tell?

"Hmm." The sound filtered through their hair, a black curtain over their face. He pulled it back and they looked up at him, chin resting on his chest.

"I'm not going anywhere yet, darling. I complain, but I reckon there's a decent number of years left in me."

They smiled, pressing their ear back down. "I know, I just like to hear you. When it speeds up, and slows down, sometimes it's a little uneven, you've got a rhythm of your own."

"I do?" He felt disarmed, very aware of his pulse the way it coursed through his body, in the fingertips of his left hand, his gut, his throat.

"Everyone is different, everyone who has one I mean. Not me." Ryoma couldn't see their expression but he could hear it well enough; another little thing that isolated them from most of humanity. He thought about their first night together and remembered the delicate sensors in his hand picking up something.

"That's not true, I know there's a little beat in here. I've felt it."

He took their hand and pressed it to their stomach lightly until he found it again. The steady pulse of their mechanical insides ticked away, a time signature he couldn't quite follow but it was uniquely theirs. "See? It's quiet but it's there."

"Oh." They whispered quietly, frowned with a concentration reserved for their piano practice, and then looked up at him. "We're in sync."

They both dozed for a few hours, taking the time to relax in each other's company and warmth as the suns began to lower their harsh gaze. When Ryoma woke up Guin was already holding a picture frame carefully at the edges.

"You meant it when you said twins huh? Practically identical." Inside was a small, ancient picture of him and his sister that he'd hung on the wall, one of the few things from his childhood he'd made sure to keep. It had been taken when the pair were rock hopping across the asteroid belt, crammed into some ancient photo booth. A young Ryo was posed next to his twin, uncomfortably trying to crack a smile despite his strong misgivings about how he looked at the time. After their parents passed, they'd been looking for a cheap way to get across the outer system, hoping to find anywhere that would let them work. Polaris had looked like a paradise then.

"Exactly identical. I think we were, what, fifteen in that picture? Think it's safe to say I look a little different now." He looked groggily at the image of himself so long ago. He'd hated having his picture taken as a kid, but he was glad he'd kept this one in the end. Looking at his reflection in the glass, the differences were subtle but they had been everything to him back then. "Being a guy suits me a little better, don't you think?"

"You do look more comfortable in your skin. It looks good on you." They smiled, pushing his unruly hair back.

"I think so too." His eyes were drawn to the picture. "It's her birthday too, Serena's. Third, no fourth one without her. Fuck. Doesn't get much easier."

"I'm sorry, I should have asked before I came here. I didn't think how hard they could be."

"The last couple of years, sure. But I'm happy you're here, I could do with a little company today. Thank you darling." He put the picture down on the bedside table, careful to face it away from the harsh glare of the suns. These things could be so easily damaged.

"What was she like? Your sister?"

"A smart-ass mainly, much smarter than me. She could weed information out of people like nobody's business."

"Bet she made for a great detective."

"Oh sure, pain in the ass quality for a sibling though. Couldn't keep any secrets from her. Boyfriends, birthday presents, there was nothing you could hide."

"You two must have had a pretty good success rate."

"We did ok. Well, I was just the muscle really, though I've not got much of that left now. We'd drifted apart for a while, once we got to Polaris from the belt, I had my boxing and that took over my life. You've got to make the best of a career like that when you can, you know? But when she was starting up this PI thing, she said she needed my help and suddenly it was like we were kids again, like no time had passed at all. We made quite a team, and I ended up quitting fighting altogether." He hadn't comfortably spoken about her for this long since she died. "She had a shit taste in decor though, the office was this corporate chic eyesore, you should have seen it. She said it made the upper-city clients feel comfortable."

"No ones perfect." That sweet little smile. "But she sounds pretty close, my brother's a similar sort."

Their brother again. They'd said he was here on Polaris, but never talked about looking for him. If only Ryoma had a name, he could probably turn something up, help them reunite. It was the least he could do. He started to ask but Guin had already gotten up to dress, grabbing a robe from the back of the bedroom door and following the trail of abandoned clothing back to the living room.

"This looks familiar," they said, attention pulled to the screen Ryoma had left running. He was so used to being home alone he'd fallen out of the habit of locking his screen. An infosec master he was not, despite his work. They peered at scans from Rearden's office. "Do you mind if I look?"

"Not at all." He followed after them, pulling in close to read their expression. Their makeshift mechanical knowledge could be useful.

"Are you thinking of getting something done?"

"Maybe, I'm just asking around." He shrugged noncommittally, unsure why he lied.

"It's strange. This is almost the exact same as my internals, in principle at least. The way it encases the brain, the patterning here, they look a little weak but it's definitely similar. I didn't think anyone made it like mine anymore."

"This is the same as yours?"

"Pretty much. You don't see anything like this outside Hephaestus, as far as I know the big two corps haven't cracked the types of processing and lifespan we have, where did you find this?"

"Some guy from the Upper was trying to sell me brainwork, I said I'd think about it."

Odd. Were the designs stolen? Copied?

"Well I wouldn't go for this, not if they're giving you incomplete mock ups. I wouldn't trust them screwing around in your head if you don't know what's going in there."

"They did say it wasn't ready for market yet. So you don't think this is any good?"

"A decade away at least, what they're trying to sell you now is a garbled mess. I'm guessing they're hoping people won't know what they're looking at." They laughed a little. "You know we had some investors buy out the club for the night a few months ago, trying to show off. One of them mentioned new age brainwork, some sleaze dressed in a vintage Terran suit that didn't fit, trying to get me to sit on his lap all night, offered me a free upgrade. Fool didn't even clock I was synthetic already. I wonder if he was selling the same thing."

The idea of them flirting in that glitzy bar sent heat pooling downward, he was still recovering but he couldn't help but tease. "I'm guessing you said no."

"I said I'd think about it. He wasn't quite my type, I think my tastes lie elsewhere." They winked, lips parted, still a little swollen.

"And who is your type?" He purred, snaking his arm around their waist. He felt them quiver a little under his hand. Still so sensitive. "You often get guys like that trying to sweeten you up?"

"On occasion." They fingered the thin chain around his neck idly. "Sometimes I get a nervous little knock on my dressing room door, the manager asks me to sit with a customer for a while, laugh at their jokes, be friendly. It can be fun, pretending. I think they get a little carried away with the fantasy of the place too. They want to woo the pretty young singer in the lounge bar, whisk me away like in those old movies." Something in the way they spoke, their voice weightless, dreamlike, suggested it was their fantasy too. Is that what they'd like? To be taken care of, protected? He could do that. He could try.

"I can see the appeal." He touched their cheek, pressing his lips to their jaw.

"Can you imagine their faces if I told them how old I was? Half of them would stroke out on the spot I'd imagine."

Ryoma laughed, looking out the window where the city below buzzed away, the faded daylight blending into the electronic artifice that kept the city alive at all hours. Guin followed his gaze, peering all the way down to street level. "You can really see where the corp's money is spent around here, it's amazing the Under staggers on."

"It's where most of my work comes from now. The law's a little thin on the ground 'less you mess with the running of things. People got to working things out between themselves."

"Yeah, that sounds like a corp colony all right." Guin's gaze turned to the sea in the distance, just beyond the edge of the city. The first sun was setting for the evening, transforming the surface into liquid chrome, disguising its usual drab murkiness. "It's been so long since I've seen the ocean. It's a beautiful view"

"It's pretty toxic now, you can barely touch it without having to take a fistful of rad tabs. You like to swim?"

"Love to." Their eyes sparkled hungrily in the light of the twin suns. "But I haven't in years. What about you?"

"I'd say yeah but," he tapped his right arm with a quiet clunk. "Not with this thing, can't get it wet."

Guin frowned. "Oh, that's not right, you should be able to. Uh, may I?" They reached out, stopping just short of his wrist.

"Sure." He held his arm out, watching them softly applying pressure along where the plates on his forearm fitted together.

"This model should be watertight, I know it. Do you mind if I look at the rest?"

"You sure this isn't an excuse to feel me up again?" He grinned impishly.

"As if I need an excuse." They arranged themself on a floor cushion in the warmth of the suns-light, their legs crossed, and summoned him down to join them. "It's easier if you're sitting."

He sat, facing away from them and felt their fingers run nimbly along the joints on the back of his shoulder, checking the seals carefully, all whilst humming, a few words occasionally breaking through. He recognized the song this time, they'd sung it the other night at the bar. Any tension in his body seemed to melt away as he listened to them work. "It's strange. Usually I hate going for maintenance."

"Maybe you just never found the right mechanic before, it's a very personal thing you know. Letting someone touch you like that, there's got to be trust there."

"Yeah, s'pose so." The pair fell silent, aside from the intimate sound of Guin's tinkering.

"The joints are loose, only about half a mil' or so." They concluded, looking at the engraving thoughtfully. "Does it ache at all, when it's raining or humid?"

"Yeah, midsummer's worst for it or whenever the weather's about to change. The joints all seize up, makes me feel like an old man." He chuckled to himself, and looked over his shoulder, where Guin was working away. They had such focus, and they touched him so carefully.

"Makes sense, moisture gets in the joints, jams it up. I bet your mechanic wants you to buy a new arm right?"

"Never shuts up about it." He shook his head. "Says the new ones are better, but I ain't convinced by his spiel. If it works, it works, you know?"

Guin laughed. "Probably gets commission on sales, I think most mechanics work that way."

"Figured it was something like that, he's always got the latest shit he's trying to push." His regular mechanic was loosely legitimate, and worked fairly quickly; which was exactly what he wanted considering how much he hated maintenance. Not a bad guy really, but he could be pushy on the upsell.

"Probably gets a discount too." They squeezed his shoulder. "Keep hold of this if you can, the newer models don't last half as long."

"Don't make them like they used to huh?" he said, only half joking.

"Sure don't. Why do you think synths started organising like we did? Corps were happy to charge us what they wanted, for components that degraded after a few years, core body parts breaking town in ten. Never mind how much work it is to adjust to a full refit, relearning how to move, communicate, just to feel at home again in your own skin, so to speak."

"Didn't think of it like that." He remembered the ache and disorientation when his first arm was bolted on, but a whole body replacement was unimaginable. "That's got to cost a bundle too."

"Yeah that's what did it. People smarter than me realised there were enough of us that we could build our own, better, bodies; ones that didn't wear down, or leave you in debt. I guess you know they didn't like that too much. The idea was that we'd set an example of what synthetics could be, how people could live. It was a nice dream I suppose."

"Heard about that when I was a kid, although I think I heard the party line when I was in school."

"You get to say whatever you want when you win." Guin huffed and went back to working on his arm. "Turns out corps didn't like synths making their own bodies, not without their input. Bad for business, apparently. When the colony council voted to run for independence, the company panicked and tried to force the factories to close first, then their private army strong-armed their way in. And corps like BioMech have way more pull than any government out here so they just absorbed it. With so little support from outside we just ran. Can't be much left of it now. Just a scoured rock."

"Are there many of you left?"

They hesitated. "There's a few around, I think. But it's a big universe, and we're spread pretty thin last I heard. I heard some had their bodies changed to be compatible with BioMech components, to fit back in, but I couldn't do it. This is mine you know? There's a few types of work people like us can specialise in, expeditions into the deep need long lived crew to keep things running, some volunteer to go. But I'm no pilot or engineer, so I'm of no value to anyone."

"You're an artist."

"And what good does that do? Compared to you, compared to anyone trying to make a change." Guin's voice hardened.

"It means a lot to me." He offered in response. Their hands stopped, resting on his steel shoulder. "What's wrong?"

"It's nothing, but this part is going to sting." They sounded genuinely apologetic for causing him any pain. Ryoma smiled, it seemed every time they met, their gentleness softened his calloused heart.

"Go ahead, I'll forgive you." He looked over his shoulder to meet their gaze until their lips brushed just barely. "But you owe me a kiss."

"I think I can manage that." They twisted his arm sharply, making Ryoma hiss through his teeth. The seal on his shoulder suddenly pinched much tighter, like being squeezed with a vice. "Shit, you weren't wrong darling."

"It'll take a few minutes or so to get used to, but it'll pass. You'll be swimming like a fish in no time."

"Probably not a fish, maybe a drowned cat." He rotated his shoulder, feeling out the resistance, the edge of his movement range. "Thank you darling. And I really mean it, about your singing. It's beautiful."

He wanted so much to say more, that they'd saved him that first night, that their songs had made him feel alive again, but the words wouldn't come.

"Thank you, Ryo. I'm happy it means something to you." Their voice softened. "That should hold for now, though you might need to re-tighten periodically. You can ask your regular mechanic, or I can do it. If you want."

"Happy to let my nurse take care of me." He turned and cupped their cheek, kissing them hungrily. They looked so beautiful, wearing a red satin robe they'd taken, loosely tied in the middle but left little to the imagination from the way the hem barely hugged their hips. An ex had left it behind, and he'd lacked the will to call them back or throw it out.

"It's easy enough." Guin smiled, looking a little coy, he had a feeling they liked him calling them that. "I do my own maintenance, and well, I'm a little more complex than you, if you don't mind me saying so."

"Course not." He was bemused at the idea of them running a full dismantle, their body broken down into lifeless static parts. "You really do your own maintenance? That's got to be pretty tough going, opening yourself up like that."

"No one knows me better than me, and I'm not so keen on strangers touching me, even though I can't do everything myself." Guin became quiet. He felt there was more to their answer, but he didn't want to pry. Most people would talk if they wanted to.

"I could help. If you tell me what to do."

"Might take you up on that. I'm well overdue for a full diagnostic, but I haven't found anyone I feel safe with in a long time."

Must be lonely, not having anyone they could trust. Outside, the evening traffic began to peak, a billion people negotiating the space just beyond the walls around them.

"I could do that, if it's not complicated." They smiled sweetly and squeezed his shoulder, sensors picking up the gentle pressure of their grip.

"Not complicated, it's just a little intimate." Their hand slid down the length of his arm, making him shiver. "We should test out your arm soon, find somewhere we can swim."

"I'd like that." He flexed his hand again, trying to think of somewhere that would still be safe. The coast was no good, it was barely safe when he went as a teenager, he couldn't imagine what it was like now, and how it could affect Guin's body. But still, with legs like that, they could have been born to it. "How about we have some dinner? I've barely eaten today, and I'm sure even you get hungry."

"Sure." Before he could stand, Guin was already up and investigating the contents of the nearly bare fridge, holding out a rapidly condensating tub of neglected leftovers. "What are these?"

"They're just some dumplings I made, I made a batch a couple days ago and sort of forgot about them. Here, I'll heat them up." He reached for the steamer under the sink. "You never had these?"

"No." They hovered at his shoulder, watching him arrange them in the steamer basket leaving a careful space between each dumpling. "I think you can tell a lot about a person by what they eat, what they cook."

Ryoma scoffed. "Well, these are about the one thing I can make. Not sure what that says about me."

"I think it says you're careful, precise. The crimping there is very neat, and it must be repetitive. You find comfort in the process." They had this way of seeing through him. A quality that in anyone else, would have annoyed him to no end.

"Would you like to go anywhere tonight? Since it's your birthday."

"I'd prefer to have you all to myself. Eat these, eat you, watch a movie." He cupped their cheek and kissed them again, savouring the taste. "Is that horribly selfish of me darling?"

They smiled and reached behind him, carefully plucking a piping hot dumpling from the steamer.

"What kind of movie?"

Chapter Thirteen

They spent much of the movie talking over the audio, Guin making comments about the surprisingly high quality of the score and laughing along with Ryo at the slapstick exaggerated violence. Guin was quickly satiated by the dumplings after only a few, leaving Ryoma with more than enough so he continued to graze until they were gone, his stomach and heart full.

He admitted to having a crush on the lead actor as a teenager, their strength and style had lit a fire in him he hadn't understood until much later. Guin had begun to imitate them in voice and manner, as he touched them. The soft curve of their spinal contacts pressed against him as they watched and he was sure he could feel their contentment radiate into him. Their robe fell open, with a little assistance, sliding to the floor. Making love came easily, holding their wrists above their head as they liked, remembering the right places to touch and kiss, a gentle bite on their nipple made them hiss with pleasure, both getting so worked up they both missed the ending.

Another time perhaps.

Ryoma was awoken by mid-morning light of the twin suns cutting through the blinds directly into his eyeline, pulling him from the pleasant quiet of dream. On instinct, he reached out to touch Guin but found the bed empty, the sensors in his hand detected the slight warmth where they'd been, his mind playing through the memory of the previous night.

Their familiar cologne clung to the sheets, a tug in his chest at their absence. A small but vocal part of him felt like one day he'd wake up and they'd be gone. He sat up, shaking the thought clear of his mind, pulled on the previous night's jeans, creased but wearable, noticing Guin's clothing was scattered on the floor. They were still here at least. Grabbing a fresh shirt from the closet, he rolled his shoulders a few times to see how it felt, newly adjusted. The movement was buttery smooth, like it had just been installed.

One hell of a mechanic.

He wished he'd known them in his boxing days, he might have won more often.

In the living room, Guin was perched on the window sill taking in the suns-light, their knees drawn up to their chest. The apartment faced the sea, it was the main reason he'd chosen it, even if it was far too expensive for the size. One of his shirts rested on their shoulders in a half hearted attempt to look decent but it still hung loose on their frame, their slender silhouette visible through the pale fabric.

"You're up," they said, eyes not leaving the horizon. "I thought I'd let you sleep, you looked so peaceful."

"Thanks, did you sleep at all?" He asked, crossing the room to join them. "Do you actually need to? I've wondered if you were just humouring me, pretending to sleep."

"Sure, a few hours. Brains need rest after all." Still, they looked exhausted, glancing at him just long enough for him to see they were troubled by something. They were playing with a small card in their hands, rhythmically flipping it over again and again.

"You don't get light like this on Scylla," they said distantly.

"No?"

"Too far from the star, it's feeble at best. Each morning feels like the sun's just about to rise, but it never does. Not quite." Remembering the week he'd spent there, Ryoma had noticed how strange it felt, like he'd never had quite enough sleep, the sky always somewhere between late evening or early morning. It likely worked in the houses' favour, a confused and drunk clientele looking to lose as much time as money in their wallet would allow.

They looked up at him, the shirt slipped from their shoulders just a touch. "I forgot how nice it can be, a little bit of sunlight."

"Maybe both of us could do with working fewer nights, huh?"

"Yeah." They shrugged, allowing Ryoma to see what was in their hands. He recognised his own name, realising on the business card he'd given them when they met.

"Is there something you wanted? My offer still stands if you want me to look into something."

Guin's lucky bet had left him with enough to live on for a little while at least, and with his arm better than ever, he doubly owed them.

"No I, I want to tell you something, I...don't really talk about it. To anyone. But we've been seeing each other, and I think you should know." They hesitated, like they were sounding it out mentally, but the words caught in their throat. "It's hard when you have to actually say it. If we were in the synapse pools I would transmit it. I could just, it makes it seem more real when you have to say the words."

They paused for a long time, clenching their jaw until the words would come.

"You've seen the scar haven't you? I've seen you looking sometimes, you're not as subtle as you think."

Ryoma looked away guiltily. "Nothing gets past you, does it?"

"It's alright, I know you didn't mean anything by it. You know what it is, don't you."

"It's a jack scar isn't it." He placed his hand on their arm.

"Jacking! I hate that fucking term." Guin hissed, turning away sharply to hide their scowl. "Being used as a doll, it's sick."

They cringed at their outburst, anxiously touching their neck. They seemed to shrink on the spot, their voice reduced to a whisper. "Sorry. It's... I can still feel it sometimes."

"No, I'm sorry. I ain't all that considerate, not so good with people when I don't have a drink in hand." Serena was the comforting type, he always stood back feeling useless when a client was distressed. But Guin wasn't a client, they needed him.

"To be truthful, I am supposed to sleep a lot more than I do, but -"

"It keeps you awake."

"It comes back to me, no matter how much time passes. It was after I ran from Polaris on some transport going anywhere and...he was like me. Naively I thought that meant he was a friend but..." They caught his eye. "You've seen marks like it before, haven't you? I can tell."

"Sure I've dealt with jac...uh cases like this." Guin's lip twitched in wry amusement at his save. He'd investigated kidnappings before, jackings of all kinds. Memories scraped out and sifted for anything of value. Colony security weren't too interested, so people like him ended up hired by the family to find the victim before the trail went cold. In the best case, they would be left with some lost time and some scarring, the worst case could leave the victim braindead.

The victim.

Guin.

It seemed so clinical, looking at them, eyes low, hugging their knees. Serena had always broken the bad news to clients, he'd never been able to face them. He tried to find the most tasteful thing to say but all he could do was stumble over a broken apology. "I'm so sorry Guin."

His heart ached, seeing them unhappy like this. He was about to reach out when they shrugged him away, shrinking into themself even more.

"It might help to talk, if you want." His voice grew as quiet as theirs.

"You a psych too, Ryo?" They took his hand and pressed it to their waist, pulling him toward them. "A man of many careers aren't you."

"No but," he tried to gather his thoughts coherently, looking into their wide watery eyes. "Sometimes, back when we had the office to work from, clients would walk in and start talking. And getting it just out to someone, they'd feel better just from talking about it. Sometimes we couldn't even help, and I think they knew, they just wanted someone to listen. People will talk if you let them, even if it's just for their own benefit."

They gave a wry smile, touching the stubble on his neck. "You're very sweet Ryo."

"In your own time, darling." He wasn't great at the comfort thing, but he wanted to try.

"I just..." Their expression hardened, jaw set. Their attention seemed to drift away, their bright green eyes becoming dull and unfocused. "I thought I'd be stronger, you know? If something happened to me. All this strength and I still froze up."

"Instinct's a hard thing to overcome darling." Not knowing what else to do, Ryoma squeezed their hand gently. "You were just trying to protect yourself."

"I suppose." They shrugged weakly, exhausted in a way he'd never seen before. A commercial transport noisily hummed as it flew past toward the 'port uptown. "Did I tell you how I ended up singing at the Reinhardt?"

Ryoma shook his head. "Tell me, angel."

"I'd been singing as I cleaned the bar one night. I thought I was alone, but the manager saw me." They smiled at the memory. "I was given the set list, and a halfway decent rental suit. I don't mind playing the same things over and over. It's like I said last night. Routines are comforting don't you think? A setlist, working a case, the structure of it. Keeps you sane when nothing else will. I know it's childish, to live in the past so, but I think I needed it." They buried their face in his neck, becoming very still, listening to his heart again. Slowly, he stroked their hair, letting the dark strands flow between his fingers.

"You survived the best way you knew how." Ryoma expected them to cry, he never knew what to do when people cried. But nothing came. Maybe they couldn't. "Besides, you managed to come and see me, didn't you?"

"You know, I was so frightened the whole flight, but I wanted to see you so badly. It's not fair of me to tell you all of this."

"Fair doesn't come into it." He looked at the business card, discarded on the window sill. "I could try and find the man that took you, if you wanted. If it would help. What he did to you is still a crime."

They grimaced, ice water dousing Ryoma's confidence. "It was a long time ago Ryo. And he's long gone I imagine, not that anything would happen if you did find him."

He knew it too, but for a moment he'd wanted to feel something other than useless. To protect them the way they'd done with him, in all the ways he'd failed Serena, and Elise Rearden. They cupped his cheek. "It's very sweet of you to offer. You're probably the first person I've been with and not had one eye on the exit the whole time. Something about you felt safe. Guess that's why I kissed you that night."

"I'm glad darling." His mind ran over their first night together; their lingering looks and gentle touches. Looking back, they had let themself be so vulnerable with him. Autumn had said something to that effect, how comfortable they'd looked with him. "I wanted you to feel good."

"You did." They murmured softly, an airy slight smile returning to their lips. He wanted to kiss them so badly. Guin's arms wrapped around him suddenly, giving him a gentle squeeze. "Thank you."

"I've got a friend staying nearby, she wants to meet you. Why don't we go out tomorrow? It's deep in the Under, synth run, and plays all sorts of music."

"A club in the Under?" They perked up in recognition.

"Yeah, you know it?"

"It's been a while but, I think I know where you mean. I liked it, I think." They smiled at the memory. "I partied a lot more back then."

"Oh yeah? I think I'd like to see that." He joined them on the window sill, pulling them in close enough that he could feel the cool seam on the back. For a while the two sat in a comfortable silence, listening to the hum of the city outside.

Chapter Fourteen

The Black Box was nestled between two much larger bars in Polaris Central. The front of the building was painted a smooth matte black, giving the sense that there was just a hole in space along the street. A single, muscular bouncer stood stiffly next to the door, tall enough they would have to duck slightly to enter, in a colour coordinated all black outfit including a high necked jacket, and dyed silver hair. They wore sunglasses despite the time, probably to hide an ocular scanner. Facial recog would throw up any obvious trouble makers, a more industrial version of Ryoma's flimsy contact.

Ryoma had arrived early and alone and now fidgeted anxiously, looked up and down the street, rifling through his jacket for his crumpled cigarettes.

Guin had gone to wander the town by themself for a few hours earlier that day. He'd tried to come with them, feeling that he should really keep them company, especially after what they'd just told him, but he was sure the last thing they needed was a washout boxer clinging to their hip. Some protection he'd be, even if something did happen. Still, the whisper of anxiety persisted. He shook his head and lit a cigarette, taking a thoughtful puff and letting his eyes shift unfocused to the bruised purple sky. What was Rearden's employer doing with cloned Hephaestan synthetics? How did the mere knowledge of that woman get his wife killed? The clicking of heels on the pavement broke through his train of thought, and brought him back to terra firma where Guin approached with a shy wave.

"There you are," he said, crushing the rest of his cigarette underfoot giving Guin's slim waist a squeeze under the loose pilot jacket they'd borrowed. "I was starting to worry."

"There's no need, I found a few places I remember and lost track of time I'm afraid." Guin pointed down the labyrinthine tangle of overlapping buildings above. "There's a neo-synthwave bar just over there, so I stopped to listen for a while. I got talking to the manager and she said there's a lounge place not that far from here."

"Huh - I never noticed that. You'll be guiding me around before long." They seemed so at home already. He showed them the way in, and Guin slipped off their coat, leaving the crest of their snake peeking out from the loose shirt that clung to their shoulders. They had a way of dressing so elegantly even in something he'd seen a million other people wear, and ended up biting his tongue for fear of saying anything that made him sound too hungry; it was still early after all.

On entry, the two of them were patted down, giving Ryoma a few seconds to scan the inside of the bar; it had been a while since he'd been here. The black and dark grey theme continued inside, minimally decorated aside from a couple booths occupied by a few fashionable socialites from the inner systems, a small dance floor with no obvious DJ, and all the way through to the back, a windowless guarded door.

"Syl should be here somewhere, ah." He nodded subtly to the woman standing at the opposite end of the bar in a pale blond fur-esque coat. Even taller than Guin, her entire body up to the throat was brightly polished steel, throwing points of light across the room. "She's a little eccentric."

He greeted Sylph with a wave and a shout, though his voice was swallowed up by the music. The woman waved back and glanced towards Guin, catching their gaze briefly. They nodded, shifting on a spot a little. Off-stage it seemed they disliked being the centre of attention.

Sylph nodded in their direction, inclining slightly. "Always nice to see a fellow synth, you don't see too many outside the Under or a gen ship."

"Same to you, I haven't seen anyone like me in a long time."

"Guin's from Scylla."

Sylph raised an eyebrow, her old friend's frequent trips to that rock made a lot more sense. "That's brave of you. It can be dangerous out there, for people like us."

"Suppose so," they said, acutely aware of that. "No more than anywhere else."

Sylph laughed. "I'm sorry, we're getting off on the wrong foot aren't we? I wrangled us a booth for the evening." Turning abruptly, she led them to an unoccupied booth in the back glancing behind her at the pair. "You two make a nice couple."

"We do," Guin agreed.

They drank and talked long into the night. Guin's initial discomfort quickly thawed as Sylph and they compared experiences, components, origins; Ryoma felt thoroughly lost but happy they got on together. Guin pulled at his wrist leading him toward the crowd of bodies on the dancefloor, they easily stood out as the tallest, most elegant.

"I'm too old to dance, angel." He stood self-consciously a few steps back from the lights. He'd been keen to come here but now he was the one who felt out of place.

"Then what does that say about me?" They murmured under the music, a hint of mischief in their voice as they pressed against his back, lips ghosting on his neck. "Am *I* too old?"

He shook his head. "Course not. You're different."

"And you like different, don't you." They spun him around, resting their wrists on his shoulders. Their lips glittered as they spoke. "Just follow me, it'll feel good."

He followed as they directed, his body theirs to manipulate, for a few songs at least until he had to pull himself away. He was after all only human, and quick to tire. On the way back to the booth he saw Sylph who had been watching them both over her drink, probably amused to see him in a good mood. It was like no time had passed at all, it easily could have been any night ten years ago, with the addition of Guin. "Tired already?"

Ryoma huffed and opened an extra shirt button wishing he'd ordered any drink other than whiskey, no ice.

"You seem very taken with them." Sylph watched him, amused.

"Yeah, they're something special." He took a drink, letting the whiskey warmth sit on his tongue. He looked over at Guin who was leaning over the bar waiting for a fresh round of drinks. They waved back at Ryo with a dreamy flushed smile.

"You love them." She wasn't asking a question, so Ryoma didn't answer. "You know Ry, people like us? We live a long time."

"What are you saying Syl?"

"You'll..." She chewed the words slowly, and he had a feeling what she was about to say. "You won't be around forever."

"I know." Of course he knew, ever since he saw that little shimmer behind their ear. Perhaps it was selfish of him, but at least they wouldn't go first. As the thought turned in his head, Guin approached with three drinks in hand and the sparkle in their eyes brighter than ever.

In the early hours of the morning, Ryoma and Guin walked back around the city, trying to keep their hands to themselves, for now at least. Colony enforcers were few and far between down here, but not non-existent. The chatter of the bar became more and more distant until only the click of Guin's heels echoed through the narrow street. "I've been thinking about you."

"Hmm?" They hugged his arm, more for comfort than need.

He wanted to ask about their life span, and what that meant for them. Would they even remember him in a hundred years? Two? Did they even love the same way? But they'd come all this way, and trusted him with their past. That had to mean something. They looked down at him with that shimmering smile, and his doubts dissolved. "Why don't you sing anything else at the bar? You seem to like every type of music there is, but I've seen you sing a lot now and your setlists are pretty fixed."

They thought for a second. "I suppose, but I always wonder if anyone would want to listen? Management would fight me for every song, I don't know if it would be worth it."

"I'm sure people would watch you regardless, I know I would."

"You're just being nice, they could replace me in a second, with a vocaloid if they wanted. It would be more consistent."

"But you play so perfectly, and that voice of yours. You could probably put the newsfeed to a melody if you wanted."

"Ryo..." They kissed him deeply, leaving a slight imprint of colour on his lips. "I...I have to go back actually, there's a private event at the Reinhardt in about thirty hours. Some mining oligarch with a fetish for the twentieth century. He wants to impress some investors, and it'll take me nearly that long to get there."

He ran his finger along his lip, examining the metallic pigment that clung. "That's a pretty tight turn around, you really wanted to see me that bad huh?"

"Don't get too smug," they smiled. "There's still a little time until my ship leaves, so we could swing by your place and then maybe you can walk me to the 'port if you're not too worn out?"

Chapter Fifteen

After seeing Guin off, Ryoma could have floated home he felt so light, their presence made him feel so alive in a way he never felt before. In such a good mood was he that he barely raised an eyebrow when he realised the elevator was on the fritz and had to take the multitudinous stairs. It gave him time to think about Guin, how they seemed so comfortable around him, and he with them. He chuckled to himself for being so far gone, a drunk old fool. If they didn't feel the same, he was fucked for sure.

With a few brief rests to catch his breath, he finally made it to his floor and immediately something felt wrong. The muffled noise of his neighbours was eerily absent and on approach it seemed his door was ajar. As he got close it became evident there were pieces of the lock littering the floor where it had been shattered. He slowed to a silent tiptoe, trying to listen for any movement inside and will himself sober, watching the thin strip of light that escaped into the hallway.

Giving the door a careful push, it swung open and he walked in, expecting the place to be trashed. But it was intact, aside from the woman sitting on his couch, drink in hand, having helped herself. The lights were off, but the moonlight cut through the half opened blinds. She wore a tailored pale blue suit and matching ponytail that stretched her face thin, a woman he'd only seen from a distance before...

"Ah, you're finally back!" She looked through to the dishevelled bedroom. "Long night I presume?"

The cuffs of her jacket were powdered with dust and debris, pieces of his door. He wondered if Guin's flight had left yet, if he could sprint back through the upper-city to join them. The twin suns rising behind them as they left for the last time, to stay in that cramped little box on Scylla. What would the consequences be if he just walked out? But he didn't move. "Ryoma LeBeau." She stretched the last few syllables, rolling the name in her mouth in a way that made him uneasy. "But it wasn't always was it?"

"The fuck are you?" He knew she was trying to piss him off, but it worked nonetheless.

"Odette Laux." She perked up in her seat and held out her hand limply, which he ignored. Shrugging at his slight, she finished her drink in a single gulp. "I believe you met some of my security detail a little over a month ago. You took my picture, and Mr. Rearden's." He remembered her hand splitting in two, the disc swallowed into the palm. "I'm assuming you tried to look me up."

He nodded, leaning back against the wall. "You're a ghost."

"So it would seem, but you've done a good job slipping between the cracks in the system too haven't you? Papers all in order I presume?"

Her words hung heavily in the air, she already knew the answer to that.

"I handle the accounts for Mr. Rearden's bosses, and their bosses too, as it happens." Her gaze lingered in cold examination, a cat watching a mouse struggle for its life. "You might have heard of them, it's their arm you're wearing after all."

He daren't say their name aloud. This was so much bigger than he thought, and a company like them had the pull to make people disappear.

"You understand, yes?" Her smile broadened. "And you understand that you've been looking into company business. So I've been tasked to come here as a courtesy."

He looked at the impact craters on the crumpled door, she was some accountant alright.

"I just follow the leads, it's not my fault where it goes."

She snorted. "But you closed your case LeBeau, paid for your services. You're a practical man, you don't work for free, why continue? Why make trouble for yourself? You've got a nice set up here, must be doing well with all those trips to Scylla, all those bars can't be cheap."

"What I do in my own time is no one's business." Resigning himself to the conversation, he picked up a clean glass for himself from the kitchenette. Any residual happiness had now dissolved, so he may as well start drinking.

"I was saving this," he grumbled, picking up the heavy glass bottle that she'd opened, and poured out a generous measure for himself.

"Hmm, in most cases I'd agree, but when you're nosing around in things that aren't your business, that's when I get the call."

"Well, unfortunately for you, that's my job." She didn't seem convinced. "What do you want then?"

"Me? I don't *want* anything, I just need you to do nothing, and my bosses' bosses' bosses are happy again. I can go home and you can continue drinking and fucking yourself to death with that robot of yours, deal?"

Ryoma stayed silent, she was trying to get him to react, make a mistake. She tapped on the tablet next to her. "I think you'll find this has been wiped. All in the cause of privacy of course, the corp needs to keep its investments safe, and if you happen to have anything else on file, we'd require that it be handed over too. The company will even give a short grace period."

"How generous." He snorted. It was nearly sunrise, the first would be up in a few minutes, the second an hour later. "You sure that's all? Don't want me to lick your boots whilst I'm at it?"

The woman barked a laugh, loud and coarse, and kicked out a foot. "Well if you're offering honey..."

"And if I tell you to fuck off?"

Her airy smile hardened, just a touch.

"There are ways to break anything Ryoma. Sure it might take some time, a little experimentation, but in the end all you need is to apply pressure in the right ways." Odette's gaze cast outward through the window, towards the spaceport where he'd left his love. "I wonder what would break you?"

Ryoma's blood turned to ice. "Get out."

The woman held up her hands and stood. "Fine, fine. I'll take my leave, I think my point has been made, don't you? You have your options."

He ground his teeth. "Get. The fuck. Out."

"Toodle-oo." The door swung behind her as she sauntered out, bouncing against the warped door frame and leaving it wide open. Her cackle drifted away with her footsteps. Ryoma threw his glass with as much force as his synthetic arm would allow, exploding against the wall in a shower of crystal.

"Fuck." He slumped to the ground and poured himself a fresh drink with the remaining glass. Then another, and another. His stomach churned with a mixture of dread and the alcohol in his system, making the expensive liquor taste like bile. It was all so fucked. He desperately wished for his sister back, that Guin could have stayed just a little longer. He wished they could have met.

Chapter Sixteen

"**I**f someone's telling you to stop, you're on to something." Serena excitedly read through the scrawled threat, slipped under the door to the office sometime in the night. She collapsed in the creaky chair, her boots resting on the desk. "Looks like we upset those corpo types."

She frowned at her brother's lack of response and turned around to see him leaning against the window he'd popped open to smoke. "I thought you quit."

Ryoma ignored her question, flipping the lit cigarette over between his steel fingers, training his fine motor control. It was a refurb and still cost more than a year's rent on this rock, but it was his own arm. No loan payments, no terms of service, it was his. Forever. Now he just needed to keep it running.

When LeBeau Investigations opened its doors he'd had his doubts that anyone would come but sure enough they did. As it turns out, the worried wealthy of Polaris will risk slumming it so close to the Under when they've got something, or someone, they want looked into quietly.

"Hey, you in there Ry?"

He looked back inside. "Huh? Yeah. I like to have something to do with my hands, it looks less suspicious when you've got me scouting places out at all hours."

"Well find something else, before you melt your lungs, jackass." She pushed an empty can across the desk for use as a makeshift ashtray. "You can't afford synthetic everything."

"I'll think about it," he said, making a show of crushing it in his synthetic hand, and letting the ash fall to the balcony below.

"Dick," she snorted, and went back to the letter. "So we're back out at the corp offices tonight, yeah? We need to get something that proves these fuckers are screwing the residents over. What's that look for?" Serena watched her brother shift uncomfortably on the windowsill.

"Threats like that thing there mean we're going to get beat up, sis. Or worse. Wouldn't it be better if we just - "

"Just what? Keep our heads down? This shit here? It's all bluster." She crumpled the note into a ball and deftly threw it into the recycler. "You worry too much for someone who used to throw punches for a living."

"That was different, Serena. It's organised, it can stop. That shit? We can't throw in the towel on that."

"So we just let people get fucked over?" Ryoma huffed, the whole point was to help people where they could, but still the danger made him uneasy. She was the only family he had. "Besides, I've seen you in the ring, you always seem to have a good read on people."

"Flatterer." Serena had never complimented his fighting before. In fact, always made a show of disapproval. Blood sports were barbaric, she said, and he was better than that. But she'd always anxiously called after each event, to check he was in one piece. "Still, I'm not sure that's quite the same though, sis. Different kind of fight."

"Sure it is." She kissed her teeth, eyeing his rumpled shirt. "So you gonna tell me why you're wearing the same thing as yesterday? And my jacket?"

"I got a lot of the same clothes and this looks better on me." He shrugged, checking his reflection in the windowpane. The satin jacket had faded after a few summers, but it still drew compliments.

"You'll have to lie better than that on the job."

"I thought I was just muscle a minute ago. But, yeah, you got me. I didn't go home last night." He pulled the window closed with a squeak. "This guy had his eye on me in the Black Box, so we went out and things just happened from there."

He neglected to mention he'd fought the same guy earlier that month in the basement of some dingy bar just before he'd decided to give up fighting for good. That he'd approached Ryoma to show there were no hard feelings for forcing him to tap out, and he had a unique way of clearing the air between them. A couple of times throughout the night.

"Of course. You've got that look." She rolled her eyes and opened a drawer in the cabinet behind her. "I finished your birthday present by the way."

She carefully tore out a page from her sketchbook, holding up a finalised drawing. Drawn in ink and some sort of shimmering foil a twin tailed lizard flowed across the page, its tails winding behind it, making a common pest look like a powerful creature of myth. "What do you think?"

"That's amazing, sis." He sat on the desk to get a closer look, admiring the brushwork under the light. "Looks like the one we had as kids, the tails..."

"Just like the one mom and dad got us, what I could remember at least. Anything prior to this is a little unreliable." She tapped the scar on her temple, memory support and fast recall. "What did we call him?"

"I remember you called it Bastard, after it bit you." A long buried memory clicked into place, no help needed. A deep well of feeling opened up inside, as he remembered his long gone birthplace. The home they'd had there. "Scrappy little critter."

"Just like you. If you want I can etch it on your new arm if you want, make it a little more special." She rotated the page in his hand. "See, it should wrap around your arm like this."

"Sis..."

"Happy birthday, Ryo."

"I didn't get you anything," he said weakly, still lost in a fog of memory.

"You can give me my jacket back for starters." He began to slide it from his shoulders when she shook her head. "Don't worry Ry. You came to help me here, that's enough. Can't be easy giving up fighting."

Ryoma shook his head. "I was getting too old for it anyway and knowing my skill set I'd just end up bouncing at some grimy night club or something. Ain't much good for anything else."

Serena laughed and looked around the office at the peeling paint. "Well if you're feeling generous you can redecorate this room for me. I'm sick of this puke green. We could do with looking more professional."

Chapter Seventeen

Ryoma took a flight to Scylla, sick of nightmares and the memory of Serena's rasping breath lurking in any moments of silence. He used his dwindling funds and left Polaris with a mind to convince Guin to come with him someplace safe, though he had no idea where. Maybe they could catch a generation ship out into the deep, they'd sleep all the way, and wake up to clean slate somewhere else. He'd done it before, he could do it again. It felt childish to run but in the back of his mind he knew just dropping the case wouldn't be enough. People like that didn't stop.

It was early evening when the ship made landfall on the gilded planetoid, the lights beginning to intensify in the gloam as he walked double time to the Reinhardt. The front of house staff seemed occupied with prepping the place for the evening so he took the opportunity to slip into the interior with a degree of confidence until he saw Guin under the lights.

There you are.

Guin was alone on the stage, playing a theme on the piano so quietly he could barely hear over the ambient noise. It was like they were afraid to play without the band, they could make themself so small sometimes. They wore a dark dress so closely fitted it could have been poured over them, their movements

155

liquid smooth and eyes almost closed as they felt out the edge of the song. With almost telepathic awareness they looked up and caught his lingering stare.

"Ryo!" Their voice barely raised, even when getting his attention they had a sense of decorum he sorely lacked.

"Guin." He smiled, even the mere sight of them lifted the weight from his chest.

They ushered him on stage, smiling with lips stained a coppery gold, barely darker than their skin.

"I'm just warming up Ry, sit down. I wasn't expecting you today." They shifted to the end of the bench to give him space, and pushed their hair back behind their ear so they could see him better. He took a seat next to them, feeling the slight pressure of their thigh against him, his eye following down to their bare foot delicately pressing at the pedals as they played.

"I thought I'd surprise you this time."

"There's plenty of time before we open. Do you mind if I keep playing?"

"Not at all." He'd not been this close to the instrument before, he felt a little intimidated, worried it might shatter if he breathed in its direction. "This thing is really something isn't it."

"It's a vintage piece, a Terran original. I try to play it as much as I can, it deserves the love so far from home." Their hands flowed over the keys almost without thought, their eyes low.

"You look amazing tonight."

"Well thank you, I like to think so," they said warmly, continuing their scales without pause. They leaned forward as if to hear the music in more detail, shutting their eyes to concentrate on the sound. Ryoma watched, wondering if he could feel like they did, so caught in the music.

"Got to say I feel really underdressed whenever I see you, I'm trying my best here." They glanced over at him, hands still occupied with the bridge section of one of their favourite songs, one the songs they hummed frequently.

"You've gotten dressed up, I see." Their gaze clung to his jacket, green leather with a loose fit, thrown over one of his newer shirts. He'd never been self-conscious about his appearance before, but Guin was so perfect he felt like a schlub in comparison. "The colour suits you beautifully, I love the pilot look on you."

"I was saving it for a special occasion, thought now was as good a time as any." Ryo shrugged, like he hadn't stood in front of the bathroom mirror on the ship, fretting about whether or not his stubble looked rugged or scruffy. Like he hadn't kept this jacket wrapped in plastic for his sister's birthday, to replace the one he'd stolen years before. Emerald green was her favourite. "I thought I should make an effort, seeing as I always get a hell of a look from the receptionist."

"Oh, yes." They rolled their eyes. "Neve's a little obsessed with 'authenticity' she calls it, thinks she's the expert on ancient Terra. We had a bit of a run in when I arrived. She tried to argue that my being a synth breaks the immersion for the customer. I think she just doesn't like full bodies. I said they wouldn't be able to find another singer for what they pay here, unless they want a cheap holo."

He snorted, taking note of the lingering looks of the other staff. Something he'd picked up on before. "What a piece of shit."

"Quite. Not that the manager cares, jittery old thing, you saw him the other week, I don't think he knows what to think of me. I only need to look the part, not be the part, so I wouldn't worry about her. Besides, people barely remember Terra here anyway, half of them have never been. They just want something that feels right, like you've walked into an old movie. It's a bit of a fool's game, authenticity, but it makes for a nice illusion, don't you think?" The piece of music they were playing made a smooth transition, the melody taking on a lively beat. They reached across and played a couple of notes slowly in front of where Ryoma sat. "Here, if you just play this here on a loop, we can play together."

"Sure, I'll try," He watched along anxiously and carefully began to tap out the keys they had indicated, conscious of embarrassing himself in front of them. Ryoma played slowly at first, pressing the keys with care. After a few bars he sped up a little, finding a comfortable pace and feeling surprisingly confident. "Never picked up an instrument before."

"You'll enjoy it, there's a little music in you I think."

"You're much better than me." They played so beautifully next to him.

"You only just started Ryo, and I've had a long time to practise, longer than you've lived I imagine."

"Then I've got some catching up to do. Maybe I'll be half as good if I keep it up."

"Everyone's got to start somewhere. Besides, it's not about being mechanically good, it's about feeling good." They paused, considering the man sitting next to them. "What makes you feel good, Ryoma?"

His mouth went dry at their low breathy whisper, and he became extremely aware of how Guin's thigh was pressed against his. "I...I used to fight, sometimes, it was better than most odd jobs on Polaris, far better than working for the corps."

"You mentioned fighting before, you were a professional?"

He met their gaze, trying to balance talking and playing with some difficulty. "Nothing like that - I mean, I did alright, mainly fought the basements of bars in the under-city, some smaller clubs in central. I wasn't anything to write home about, but I could always read my opponent pretty well. People telegraph their moves more than they think, there's a sort of rhythm to how people move."

"Like a dance." Their eyes lit up. "So there *is* music in you."

"Yeah, yeah something like that, the back and forth, even how people breathe, everyone moves differently. You've just got to work backwards and find what trips them up." He smiled, cautiously trying to improvise, much to Guin's delight. Their bare ankle brushed against his. "Bought this arm with my winnings, just about destroyed my previous one to get it. I didn't want to get stuck on a credit plan, even if I lived in a crappy box room with no windows for the rest of the time."

"Good investment, it's a beautiful piece. And I'll bet all that people-watching that carried well into your new career. Being able to read people like that, tracking people's lives, the patterns people move in."

"Sure, when I'm focused at least. Feels like I'm pretty out of practice nowadays, but you probably figured that out from the mess I was in when we met, huh?"

"Maybe you need something to help you focus."

He took his eyes off the keys to watch them play. "I get distracted easily, especially now that I work alone."

"Am I a distraction?" They smiled coyly, improvising a little solo, running in circles around his bass notes. His heart fluttered as they cupped his chin and kissed him, still playing with their free hand.

"The best kind."

Leave with me.

There were regular ships leaving the system, he'd checked. Sylph could fudge their papers, get them on some generation ship, just leave everything behind.

"Should you be working right now? It feels like you haven't mentioned work in a little while. Not since your birthday at least."

"It's still in progress." He thought about his kicked-in door, and Odette's warning. "I've stalled a little on this one, if I'm honest darling. So I thought I'd take a break, clear my head, and it gives me a chance to visit you." The winnings from their first night together were rapidly running dry, multiple round trips to Scylla were beginning to bite financially. He'd have to think about a new case sometime soon. He wasn't even being paid for this one, and the cost could be steep. If they were hurt or worse, he didn't know what he'd do.

"Lucky me, maybe you should take a break more often." They continued playing, improvising liberally, until the nervy manager appeared and asked them to keep it down. Guin watched him leave, and then continued as before, indicating to Ryo he could do the same. "I've been thinking, it seems like quite the career move, from boxing to detecting...detective-ing?"

"Says the musical mechanic," They both laughed a little. "Like I said, I wasn't anything special, was never gonna go that far." His hand slipped, a discordant note rang out around the club and he whipped his hands away from the instrument, embarrassed to have sullied it.

"Fuck, sorry."

"That's ok, keep going if you like." They continued without missing a beat. "See? Nothing lost. You can always start again."

He regained his composure, and began. After a few bars he settled back into the flow. "Serena, my sister, she got her PI licence, said she needed some help, and I figured I'd be of much more use. And, she helped me a lot early on. When we were kids and I was still figuring myself out, I figured I owed her that much."

"It's sweet of you to continue her work like that."

That's what Sylph said, that's what everyone said.

"I try to keep it going. Not sure it's what she would have wanted." He wondered what family was like for Guin. Perhaps things are different when you're ageless, parting for long stretches but always returning. What about their brother, did they miss him? His train of thought was broken by a peck on his cheek, the assorted rings and jewels hanging from Guin's ear softly jangled, colours shifting from blue to green to pink.

"I'm sure she'd want you to be happy, Ryo. Whatever you do."

"Yeah," He watched them play for some time, remembering Odette's threat, and felt that weight on his chest return. The past few days he'd been plagued by a sinking feeling he'd lose Guin too, sooner or later. Like his parents, his home, Serena.

He stopped playing.

"Could you sing for me? Anything you like, I just want to hear you." They searched his expression, smiling anxiously, like they could sense he wasn't happy.

"Of course my darling, how about this?" They'd never called him that before. The piano fell silent for a second, the final notes slowly fading into the general chatter of the staff milling around until they were nothing, and a beat later the room filled with sound. Languid and winding, it was unlike anything they'd played before; the time signature was strange and initially hard to follow but after a few bars he had an ear for it, another of Guin's little idiosyncrasies he was privy to. Their sonorous voice filled the spaces between the notes, the lyrics sliding between old Terran and Polaris dialect, he couldn't understand it all but he could feel it well enough. Like the hushed echo of waves that draws him towards the shore, calling him into the sea. When the song ended, they let the last few notes ring out into nothing, even the background hum of the bar seemed to have disappeared.

"Do you like it? I wrote it for you." Guin rested their head against his shoulder. "I haven't written anything in a long time."

He squeezed his eyes shut to blink away the threat of tears. "I ... I don't deserve you."

"I hope it's not too much." They ghosted their fingers along the keys, working through the movements for another few bars. "I haven't had much chance to practise yet, I'm not sure of the melody."

He touched their wrist, wishing there was a way to stay in this moment. "It's perfect

Ryoma was pinned against a cold metal floor, his body felt weak and restrained, but also sickeningly wrong. He felt stretched, his limbs unwieldy and unresponsive. He tried to calm his mind, to remember how he got here, and figure out how he could escape. Through the floor he could feel the characteristic low rumble of a sub-light drive, from his limited field of view the room seemed small, cramped, passenger quarters perhaps, but his line of thought was interrupted by a door opening and closing behind him.

"Let me go!" He tried again to move, but this ersatz body refused. His voice felt alien in his mouth, the pitch was off, the sound warped.

"Shut it up before people hear." A voice above him hissed, someone other than the person holding him still.

"Coming up..." The person restraining him was bored, this was routine. Ryoma tried again to push back against what restrained him but a hand pressed his face into the ground and yanked the collar of his shirt down. Something sharp penetrated the back of his neck into his spine, making him yelp. There was a brief searing pain, and he felt something cold invade his body, trickling through his nervous system like ice water.

The sound of fabric tearing, and the chill of recycled air on his back. A hand slithered along his spine and tilted his head to look behind his ear. Ryoma grew sick as they touched him, in this skin that felt like it was someone else's, wishing he could just make himself move. A device pinged faintly.

"You were right, full body through and through. Exactly what we needed." He was roughly rolled over and propped up against the wall, now too limp to resist. The room had a loose feel to it, it had no edges but still felt claustrophobic, the faces of his captors were a featureless fleshy smear, everything out of focus. Nonetheless, he could still feel the way he was being leered at. Ryoma tried again to speak, even if only to spit obscenity, to resist at all in any way, but his jaw felt wired shut.

"Yeah that's what it told me." The man across the room said, his voice dropped in volume as he conferred with someone over comms. "Boss says to bring it in."

"Good." The figure loomed over him, very close now. Touching his cheek. Warm breath. "Kind of pretty too. I wonder if I can keep it after they're done." Ryoma tried to shout again but was only able to murmur thinly. "Don't look so scared, little doll."

Stop, stop, stop, stop.

"You're disgusting, c'mon let's move it."

Ryoma woke with a gasp, clammy and cold, hurriedly checking he had control of his faculties. He took a few breaths, squeezing his fists open and closed then scrambling at the ghostly burning on his neck for a puncture wound. Nightmares weren't unknown to him but this was different, far more intense than anything he'd experienced before. There was a sickening chill when he'd been touched, and he felt the overwhelming need to scrub himself clean.

Next to him Guin had rolled over and was watching him, worried. They were easily woken up at the best of times. "Ryo, what happened? Are you ok?"

"Sure, sure. It was just..." He ran his hands through his hair, feeling his animal fear dissipating with every breath. "Just a weird nightmare, really fucked up, really vivid."

"Oh." They sat up, fiddling with the chain around his neck but careful not to touch. "What was it?"

"I was attacked and these guys, vultures maybe, had me pinned down. Stuck me in the neck."

Guin froze, their face washed of colour, their eyes panicked and glassy. "Did, did one of them call you a doll?"

Ryoma tried to think, the memory of the dream was rapidly evaporating, as they often did, but that part still clung like sticky fragments of a spiderweb.

Little doll.

"Uh yeah. That's pretty creepy, how did you know that? They said something about a full-body too. Reckon I must have been thinking about you, or the case, or something." He was about to laugh it away but the fright in their eyes and the specificity of their question told him something wasn't right. "What is it, darling?"

"I didn't tell you that." Their eyes were wide with panic. "I never..."

"Tell me what?"

"Doll." They touched the back of their ear, shaking their head. "Transference shouldn't be that strong, it shouldn't..."

"Guin?"

"You don't have any brainwork like I do, you shouldn't experience memory-seep like that."

His stomach dropped. The neck puncture. "Memory...that was you? That's what they did?"

"The contact seams. When we touch, sometimes things can slip through. Usually it's just feelings, warmth but... it can be more. I, I didn't want you to see me like that...I didn't." Retreating from him, Guin hugged their knees, and fell unnaturally still. Not even a panicked breath or tears, it was like someone switched them off. "I'm not a doll."

"Of course not." Slowly, he reached out and slowly touched their shoulder, giving them time to refuse if they wanted, and kissed the contact behind their ear. "No one's going to touch you like that again. I promise you."

"I thought this time would be different, and you wouldn't see. Everytime I try to get close to someone it sort of slips out."

"It's happened before?"

They nodded. "They'd say it was ok, but they'd never look at me the same. Seeing the scar's one thing, but seeing it happen... I guess it doesn't sit right." They pressed their forehead into the crook of his neck, head bowed, like they couldn't bear to look at him. "It's ok if you want to go."

"Don't talk like that darling, it was an accident." He tilted their head up until their eyes met. "I won't leave you, and anyone who did ain't worth your time."

"I don't know what you must think of me, used like that." It hurt him that they really thought of themself that way. Used. Useless.

"I think you're much stronger than me, there's nothing could make me think any less of you." He kissed the scar on their neck and pulled them close into his embrace, feeling the chill of their spine against his chest.

They sat for sometime in the dark, quietly feeling each other's warmth, but Ryoma's brain ticked away, the connection between them and the Rearden case was looking stronger every time he thought about it. Guin's attackers had said something about them being a synth, why were they looking for them specifically?

They wouldn't puncture someone just for a quick fuck.

Guin stirred in his arms as if to remind Ryoma who this affected and felt repulsed at his thoughts. He remembered the feeling of their terror that gripped his entire being, frozen whilst his mind screamed at him to struggle, shout, do anything. Had he always been like this? Blunt, inhuman. The world was tough and he'd toughened himself against it, too much so, and left himself cynical and lonely, even before Serena died. How did Guin stay so gentle when they'd lived so much longer? They had no reason to take him in on the night they'd met, but they'd helped him all the same. They wanted so much to trust even after they'd been burnt.

He thought about the Raxle scans Guin had seen, a weak facsimile of their own brainwork. Outsourcing the more illicit research wasn't unheard of, using desperate people to test new synthetics and software that needed human trial. But what happened to Guin; kidnap, memory scrape, and whatever that sick fuck did to them. This was far worse, it had to be related somehow. He wanted to bounce the idea with Guin, see what they thought but he didn't want to upset them further, when they seemed so calm in that moment.

He began to wonder if anything of his past had ever slipped into their dreams, unknown to either of them. "Did anything of mine cross over? Nothing so intense, I would hope."

"Yeah," Guin nodded, their head resting on his stomach, listening to his heartbeat. "I was in a little apartment, just a living room really, and it was raining too. It felt like it always rained. I was with your sister, I recognised her from the picture at yours, and I'm guessing parents. They'd brought home a twin tail for your birthday. You two were so happy, it was very sweet."

Ryo's chest tightened at the memory of that place. Some half terraformed mining rock in the asteroid belt with no formal name outside of a lengthy cartographer's designation, he'd made a point not to remember it. Rain was a permanent fixture, pattering on the thin metal roof of every building, running down the drains, nothing was ever quite dry. "You'd both always wanted a pet to play with and teach tricks. You didn't have your arm back then."

His synthetic palm itched. "Yeah, that sounds right. There were no animals where we grew up, just rain and sludge, barely an atmosphere. The guy who sold them said they were exotic, never mentioned they were common as mud just two day's travel away."

Not long after he and his sister had been orphaned, the entire rock was 'dissolved,' broken up into raw material by the corp that owned it, turning the pair out with a measly credit payout as compensation, just enough to get them one-way to the nearest settlement. He couldn't remember what happened to the twin tail. "They did their best."

"I'm sure they did, I could feel how much they loved you. Your parents."

"Yeah? You could feel that?" Ryo pulled them closer.

"You get a feel for it after your first few dives. Love." They looked up at him, pulling him toward their lips.

"Yeah?"

"Did you realise your sister was letting you win? When you played Galaxy Quake together. There were a lot of easy wins she let you take."

"Huh, I didn't." She still had a way of surprising him, even after she was gone. "We drifted apart once we got to Polaris, only really got close again when she started the business a few years back. Suppose I'm glad of that at least."

"She loved you very much Ryo, I wish I could have met her."

"Me too."

"Maybe if I sing for both of you, she'll hear." They looked at the time softly glowing on his wrist. "Oh, it's so late, don't you want to try and sleep?"

"No, I'm awake now darling. Don't suppose you need any either do you?"

They shook their head and gazed up at him. "Can you stay here tonight? I haven't got a set tomorrow. We can stay in bed."

Who could ever leave you?

Chapter Eighteen

Ryoma stayed that night, and the next day too, in no hurry to return home if he could still call it that. After the break in, the apartment felt sullied, and it was likely being watched by the corps to boot. Guin stayed close to him, deep in thought all morning speaking very little and resting their head on his chest, until he finally surrendered to the need for the bathroom. He figured he was up now and made coffee for them both and put food down for Perci so Guin wouldn't have to. As he watched the coffee drip into the jug below, he enjoyed the quiet domesticity of the moment, the cat's gentle purr as she ate, the quiet rustling of sheets through the door.

As he handed them a cup, they flashed a smile from behind their sweep of hair, lips forming the beginnings of words. "I want to show you something about myself, something I've not shared for a long time. I hope that's alright."

"I... sure." Anticipation bubbled in Ryoma's chest. He wondered what Guin could mean, and if there could ever be anything they did that he wouldn't accept. "What is it?"

"It's, it's what makes me different from others. I don't think so many people know what a synth like me looks like, not really."

Entranced, he watched them kneel on the bed, their spine flexing like liquid as they moved. They took his hand and pointed to a couple of places on their torso, just above the hip and the shoulder on the opposite side. "If you could press down, here, here, and here."

With a stretch he was able to press the indicated points on their skin, which impressed with an almost silent click. Guin's torso stiffened as though a current was run through it and thin cracks appeared along their body. Segments of their skin had split, separated into evenly sized plates, one on their back, two on their front, reaching from throat to waist.

They took his wrist , pressing his hand to the newly created seam that bisected their chest. "It just lifts away, doesn't take much"

Their voice had shrunk to a soft whisper, their two tone eyes looking down at him with hope, trying to disguise their nervous energy. They wanted him to undress them, in a way. Despite everything they still allowed themself to be vulnerable.

With extreme care he lifted away the outer layer of their back. It was likely extremely tough, but he was convinced it might shatter like porcelain in his clumsy, painfully human hand. There was a slight resistance before it gave way, as though the piece was magnetised but when it did, he was surprised by how lightweight it was, not much thicker than organic skin. But that was nothing compared to what was underneath. Ryoma was lost for words, staring at the beautifully arranged fabric of multi-colour circuits and wires, the hardware woven together beneath a transparent casing. Something like glass tinted a pale grey-purple, like an overcast morning. Some sort of poly-plastic far more advanced than anything he'd ever seen before, sleek, smoothly designed. Beautiful.

Guin removed the rest of the plating, uncovering their arms to show the full extent of their insides. They pointed to the arrangement of wires and circuits blinking inside their chest, his eye naturally following them flow down the length of their body, like veins and arteries disappearing and reappearing.

"It's all in here, see? All the major processing power, cooling, oxygen supply to my brain, what there is of it at least. It's, it's not too strange for you is it?" Their mismatched eyes flitted to him, searching his expression presumably for disgust but all they saw was his wonder.

"It's like glass, I've never seen anything like it. May I?"

They nodded, and, afraid of breaking something, he placed the synthskin segment down with a clink, noticing the maze of sensors on the inside of the piece. He looked back at them, still trying to make sense of what was underneath. Engraved into their chest was the same serpent as above, embossed into the surface, still glowing just slightly. He ran his fingers over the texture, down the soft swell of their chest to their clear, smooth stomach, indented in place of a belly button. "It's beautiful, you're beautiful."

"Don't put me on too high a pedestal Ryo, you might not be able to reach." They pushed his hair back, watching his admiration with amusement. "Are you blushing?"

"I feel like I'm seeing you naked for the first time, like truly." He pressed his lips to their stomach, feeling it jolt just a little. Just a reflex.

"You've seen me before, baby."

He shied at the pet name. "Not like this I haven't, it's incredible. How you fit so perfectly. It's really something else. Does all of your, uh, detach like that?"

"My face plate is fused," They slid a finger along their jawline. "It's a difficult piece to remove unless I really have to, lots of moving parts, but most comes away. Here see?" They fidgeted to their knees and indicated to a similar set of indentations on either hip. "You know I never used to wear all this, all the time. It's like an extra set of clothes. But I was afraid to stand out, after everything."

With a click they detached the rest, adding each piece to the neat stack at the end of the bed. They stretched their newly bare legs like a person freed from a stifling room, flexing their toes. "What do you think?"

They looked at him expectantly but Ryoma's attention was drawn to their reflection in the mirror. From the base of their skull, thin hairline cracks spread across the casing on their back; Threads like spider's legs stretching outward across their narrow shoulders and down their back, around their spinal contact seam and finally fading to invisibility just above their waist.

"It's bad, isn't it?" Their voice fell uncharacteristically flat, devoid of their usual melodic tone.

"Sorry, I didn't mean to stare."

"No please." They caught his metal wrist, and looked at him pleadingly. "Tell me what it's like. I've been scared to look."

Ryoma positioned himself behind them and delicately pushed their hair aside to get a better look at the damage. Something had punctured their neck above the top of their contact seam, and judging by the impact, it had gone all the way through the skin, and the toughened internal casing, into where he guessed their brain stem would sit.

Agony.

His stomach tightened. He'd dealt with violent cases before, people who'd been hurt, attacked, abused. He'd always had the luxury of distance. Guin had been right when they first met, it could be rough out here.

"Ryo?"

He'd been silent for too long.

Stumbling, he tried to explain what he could see, running his fingers along the cracked surface, causing Guin to flinch. "Shit sorry, there's, there's a lot of fracturing on the surface, I'm not sure how much damage there is."

They turned, looking at their reflection with a look of resignation. "I could feel it when it happened. Like a window cracking. I knew, I just didn't want to see."

"I'm so sorry."

"I don't know why I didn't just..." Their voice faltered.

"Things like that, you can't control how you'll react." Ryoma's jaw tightened. Telling them not to blame themself, as though he doesn't do that everyday.

What a joke.

"I'm sorry, it's selfish of me." They recovered their composure a little. "Wallowing like this. Hiding away."

Ryoma cupped their cheek, pressing his forehead to theirs. "It's not. I think you deserve a little time to wallow, until you're ready."

"We'll just have to take care of each other, won't we?" They interlaced their fingers with his.

"Yeah, we will." His hand was drawn to the centre of their chest, the casing had looked solid but had a gentle give, like taut muscle. "You said you needed diagnostics, right? That you were overdue? I could do that, since you're undressed and all."

"If it's not too much trouble."

"Not at all." He wanted to say he'd do anything for them at this point, but he hesitated, and the moment was gone.

Guin nodded and began searching through the back of the wardrobe, behind suits, dresses, jumpsuits and jackets they recovered an ancient looking tablet, it's thick case had seen far better days. They began to explain the diagnostics process, their mood lifted with a task to focus on, and although most of the details went straight over Ryoma's head it seemed similar to what his mechanic had run on his arm, just scaled up to a full body. Shut down, scan, reboot. Easy. Except they were unconscious for the process. Just like falling asleep, but he could see how it would make them feel unconscious.

"That's really it?" He asked, trying his best to not be distracted by their body, the way it caught the light, their broad shoulders and soft hips. He was glad not to have to do anything complex.

"That's all there is to it baby..." They sang it like a lyric, brushing a knuckle down the chain on his neck. "Just make sure I wake up, ok?"

"Ok." Part of him had been expecting to perform something far more elaborate, but just watching them sleep felt like he wasn't helping at all. But still their life was in his hands. "You could ask anyone to do this, you don't need me."

"But I don't want anyone else. I trust you." He could see in their eyes they meant it, though he had no idea what he'd done to deserve their trust.

Guin lay back on the bed and began the power-down process, clipping a tablet to a hidden outlet on their wrist. He stayed next to them, dressing in yesterday's clothes and perching on the edge of the bed next to them as they fell deathly still. Unsure what else to do, Ryoma waited anxiously by them, never wandering more than a few feet away, and occasionally checking the battered old tablet plugged into a small outlet on their wrist. As if he understood anything on the screen. Nothing beeped or blinked for attention, only the progress bar tick slowly up. Probably a good sign. Probably. His hands began to itch, as his cravings began to get the better of him, so he popped the slender bedroom window to smoke. Looking down at them, so quiet and still, he thought better of it, and settled to rolling his last cigarette between his fingers until it fell apart.

Still, he needed something, the ache in his eyes making him keenly aware of how little he'd slept in the past few days. But he couldn't miss anything. Waiting for a fresh coffee to brew, he took a closer look at the beach pictures on their wall. In the distance was a much smaller Polaris Central, the few skyscrapers standing lonely against the suns, the industrial blocky housing clustered around them. In the foreground the beach stretched on and on at low tide, black sand rapidly drying under the twin suns. Polaris was lucky in a way; it had started as a company colony, not much different from the rock he grew up on, but the mineral deposits were much larger, and worth the effort to excavate. Large enough to settle. Now it was the centre of the Outer system territories.

SW-986.

The name of his home planet sprang back to him from whatever crack in his memory it had been hidden. Everyone just called it a rock, because that's all it was in the end. After it was gone it seemed to have completely fallen out of public consciousness, the most he'd ever found about it was a single line in a newsfeed stating it had been scoured, cored like an apple. Whenever people asked where he was from, they never knew it. Eventually he stopped saying, to avoid the inevitable conversation, letting people guess based on the under-city accent that had taken hold over the years.

Sometime later, a soft shuffle of movement came from the bedroom. Guin was awake.

"Hey you." He sat at their side and helped them sit up, still half asleep and leaning heavily on him for support. He passed them the tablet after giving it a pass, as if it would suddenly make sense to him. "Here, hope this means something."

"Thank you." Their voice was thinner than usual, like they hadn't quite finished powering back up. Guin detached themself from the tablet and frowned at the screen, scrolling and tapping to interrogate the numbers further. "It's what I thought, I really need a proper strip down."

"Is that bad?"

"I knew it had to be done eventually, I can't maintain everything by myself forever. Just thought I had a little longer is all." Disappointed, they put down the tablet. "Don't know why it bothers me so much, it's just routine. Just don't like the idea of people rooting around in my head, again."

"Well, I don't mind keeping you company if it helps. I can be your chaperone, of sorts."

"I think it might, I always seem to feel better with you." They smiled, touching his lip with a cool transparent hand. They started and made a grab for the neat stack of plating next to the bed. "Sorry, I should probably cover up, this is probably a little much."

"No need to be sorry, I actually..." His gaze lingered, and he leaned forward to kiss the spot on their jaw that gave way to their transparent inside. "You look good like this."

"I think so too," They crossed their long legs, posing demurely, which only succeeded in drawing his eye downward. "Feels like I have nothing to hide, it's just me."

He felt very overdressed next to them, even in just the shirt he'd thrown on against the cold. He wanted to shed like they had. Ryoma knelt on the floor before them, gripping their slender hips and kissed their stomach just below the end of the serpent's tail.

The clear surface of their body yielded to his touch just a little, they even felt warmer like this. The delicate moving parts inside Guin ticked softly, tiny green lights pulsing like breath, an impossibly complex system he couldn't ever hope to understand. He kissed lower until his mouth found the familiar warmth between their legs, and sucked on the hardened bud of their clit. Always so sweet for him. "Are you more sensitised like this?"

"Uh huh." They nodded weakly and propped themself up on their elbows to watch him, eyes half lidded and mouth open. Any self consciousness they had felt seemed to have evaporated around him. The low, cool lights from outside made their body sparkle in the semi-darkness, shifting as they moved, hips bucking in need for more. "I, please... "

"Just when I thought you couldn't get more beautiful." He climbed on top of them, pulling his shirt over his head, desperate for closer contact. It was like rediscovering their body for the first time, their true self and his. "Are you sure you're not a siren? Some trickster, a fox stealing my virtue?"

"Virtue? Have you got much of that?" They tugged at his belt with the same need to see more, feel more.

"Not really." He slid easily into them, drinking in their moans.

"And would you stop if I were?" Guin shivered under him, crossing their ankles around his waist and pulling him in deeper until he shuddered.

"Not a chance darling."

Chapter Nineteen

Ryoma woke to the ear bud chirping incessantly, whatever time it was it was too early. He groaned and hung up to doze for longer. Guin was already up as usual, the trickle of hot water combined with the drifting smell of coffee reassuring him of their presence. Still here. Almost immediately it began ringing again which he continued to ignore for as long as he could bear until he surrendered with a huff and tapped the bud to receive.

"Finally." The voice at the other end was less than impressed.

"Sylph?" He sat up, trying to bring himself to full alertness. Through the doorway he could see Guin crouched on the floor to feed Perci, still stripped of their plating from the throat down. They caught his eye and smiled, looking down and imitating the cat's meows as they put the food bowl down. "It's still early here, what's going on?"

"Please, it's almost midday where you are. It's about this case. I found something, it's... you'll want to look at this. I don't think I should talk on here."

"The case? That was nothing, I'm..."

Running away.

"I was imagining things, Syl. Overworked. I was wrong." He lowered his voice, in the hopes Guin didn't have any enhanced hearing on top of everything else. He wanted nothing more than to give them the quiet life they deserved. He could set up shop on Scylla. Specialise in background checks, stay off the radar.

"But you weren't. You were right, Ryo." There was an urgency to her voice he'd never heard before, it really was serious. "Something really fucked is happening to people like me, like your friend, and I think your mark from Scylla is the weak link."

"Fucked how?" He sat up, feeling a dull ache where his ribs had almost healed, but not entirely. Fractures need time. There was no delay in her responses, she must be close. "Wait, where are you?"

"It doesn't matter. Meet me in the Platinum tonight, I'll tell you where to find me."

"You're on Scylla too?" She'd already hung up. He tapped the bud again but the line was closed. "Shit."

"What's wrong, Ry?" Guin stood in the doorway, searching his expression. Ryoma has no idea how much they'd heard.

"Sylph called. A case. There's been a breakthrough I think." He considered the possibilities, wondering what the hell Sylph meant. People like her and Guin. Odette knew about them, maybe they were on BioMech's system somehow. If she knew that, they'd never be safe even if he dropped it. "Do you feel like a trip to Platinum tonight? What are the suites like?"

"Pretty expensive, usually full of tech oligarchs with more credits than sense." Guin's nose wrinkled in disgust, not their scene. They picked up Perci who'd become increasingly vocal at the lack of attention. She immediately calmed in their arms, looking up at them wide eyed and purring. "I can take you there, if you want."

Somewhere crowded, heavily staffed. No one could get to them there. "Yeah, you can show me the way."

"Okay, but I'll put my plating back on." They indicated to their bare body under the shirt. "Otherwise we'll spend the night dodging chasers with a fetish for visible hardware.

Later that night they headed out, Guin led the way towards the main strip although Ryoma knew it too. He'd spent most of the day contemplating what could be so urgent but so dangerous that Sylph couldn't tell him in a call, even briefly considering just bundling Guin onto a shuttle out of here, telling them to wait for him. Somewhere secret. Somewhere safe. There were enough cracks in the system to hide if needed, the craggy reef of the under-city allowed for it.

As they arrived at the Platinum, Ryoma's ear bud chirped but before he could say anything, Sylph's voice cut through the chatter. "Come to the private suite at the back."

The feed disconnected so abruptly, he wondered if the signal was jammed. "You know the way to suites?"

"Sure it's through here." Guin led the way, brushing their hand against his. They made a beeline through the casino floor toward the lounge. "I've been here once or twice."

"Oh?"

"I'm not allowed on the casino floor but, I've been here as a guest," they said cryptically.

Inside the VIP suite, Sylph had a grim look about her, far removed from her usual demeanour. Something was wrong.

"How did you manage this?" The plats' always booked out for months." Guin seemed more bemused than anything, they didn't know Sylph well enough to see when she was serious.

Ryoma stood uncomfortably against the wall, the location set him on edge already and Sylph's expression made his gut churn.

"This was nothing. The booking system is barely locked and ghosting a payment is child's play. You know, *hacker crap*." She winked at Ryoma. "This, on the other hand, was pretty tough to crack Ryo. I wanted to meet somewhere independent, where the corps won't see or track."

"So you got in right?"

"Eventually. I looked into Raxle's servers, and they had some dark stuff on there." She sighed, her eyes glued to Guin. "Ryo, you were right, this is much more than a guy cheating on his wife you know?"

I shouldn't even be here.

"So what did you find?" He noticed her glancing at Guin.

"There's memory skims from synthetic brain work, ripped right from the buffer, but there's also a catalogue of half complete body blueprints. Hey, take a look Guin, see what I'm saying?"

Guin inspected it with a frown. "This is...this is all wrong. If these are meant to be synth brainwork the connections are a mess. Cascade would be inevitable. It'd only be a matter of time before they needed a full reset, this could cause permanent brain damage, a stroke, who the hell is building bodies like these?"

"You said the same about those Raxle specs." Ryoma looked over it too, with a creeping feeling he knew where they were from. "Or near enough."

"Is this where they got them?" Guin's eyes were fixed to the scans, with a look of recognition they touched the screen. "Maybe they polished it up, tried to reverse engineer it from what they had."

"I think so, I think it's to do with this," She tapped at the screen, displaying a frozen video. The resolution was poor but it was an overhead shot of someone slumped forward in a chair, enough to see a familiar puncture in their neck. "There's some footage of the process too, a demonstration of sorts, this was the earliest I could pull." Her voice flattened to a monotone, the usual liveliness in her voice gone. She let the feed run.

The angle of the camera meant all that was visible was the steel floor, and small table of surgical implements. Gloved hands, a med-mech of sorts, inspected the victim's neck, already punctured through the skin. There were some voices in the background, something about a neural shunt, a clean scrape. The mechs hook their captive up to a thick, grey cable that leads away beyond the reach of the camera, making them twitch.

"Looks like they shut down the higher brain function to run it. They're still awake, but they can't move. "

Ryoma wasn't sure at first, the captive was faced away from the camera to show the shunt in their neck but as the clip rolled on, they twitched enough for him to see the bump in their nose, the distinct seams behind their ears.

Guin.

"That's enough of that," Ryoma said, leaned forward, abruptly cutting off the video. The three stood in silence for some time.

Sylph knew it too. "Guin, I..."

"Did they do this to a lot of people?" Guin asked, voice tight and controlled.

"It's likely, there were a lot of references in the database, it covers a couple of decades at least, going back to the fall of Hephaestus. I'm pretty sure they're all different individuals."

"How....how many do you think?"

"Maybe a hundred recorded scans. Anyone like us or near enough would have been susceptible."

"No one noticed this was happening," Guin said weakly. "No one at all."

"It's a big galaxy out there, few people go missing, won't raise any alarms unless it's someone important."

"No one came looking for them." Barely a whisper behind him. He reached back to grasp their wrist but his hand found nothing but empty air. The door behind them swung shut.

"Shit," he hissed. "Sylph I have to..."

"It's ok, go!" She urged, deactivating her tablet. "Just find me later ok?"

"Sure." Ryoma made his way through the casino floor, shoving through the teeming mass of tourists and socialites, trying to make it to the exit and find Guin before they disappeared entirely. He couldn't leave them alone, not now. Losing someone else wasn't an option. Outside it was icy cold, the breeze cutting him to the bone. Above the crowd he spotted Guin just as they disappeared around a corner, their pace much faster and a full head taller than everyone else, and the distinct click of those silver shoes on the ground.

He strained to pick out the sound of them from amongst the noisy evening crowd, and he wondered how many of the people were wearing synthetics built from scraped blueprints, stolen parts. Brainwork was complex, they wouldn't have started there. His chase led him into an alley just off the main strip, where he found Guin slumped on the ground, just wide enough for them to sit with their legs stretched out, staring vacantly into nothing.

"Darling?"

"I'm sorry, I shouldn't have come. I'm not built for this," they said weakly, hugging their arms. He sat next to them on the cold concrete.

"You're ok, it's over now." He touched their wrist, trying to bring them back like he had before.

"I just wanted it to stop, I could feel it the whole time." Their voice quavered as they spoke, they hadn't heard him. "He wouldn't stop."

"No one's going to hurt you anymore."

"You can't promise that, Ryo."

"You're right, but I can try."

"Ryo, we have to stop this, we have to..." Guin snapped to attention, looking down the alley. Something shifted in at the gloomy end of the street, the shuffling of feet trying to be quiet. They were being watched. "Someone's coming."

"I heard it too, let's go."

"What about your friend?" They looked up at him as he stood, taking his hand even though they didn't need it.

"Syl's smart, she'll have left already. Come on, I'll take you home. Let's take the long route."

They hurried in the opposite direction, Guin leading him on a complex route that zigzagged through the city, making light work of the labyrinthine streets. But as they approached the outskirts of the main strip a familiar figure appeared, the heavy who'd followed him from the Satellite, with two new companions in tow.

"We've got to stop meeting like this." The man grinned at Ryoma, ignoring his companion entirely. He'd had his nose reset since they last met. "Warning wasn't enough for you?"

A hand clamped around Ryoma's throat, lifting him from the ground, beginning to winch shut around his windpipe. His vision began to blur as he clawed and kicked in vain, when he was suddenly released, gasping. The man crumpled to the ground, completely limp, a thin line blood ran out of his mouth. Guin stepped over him to offer Ryoma a hand, snapping the other two men a look so deadly that they scattered.

"Is he dead?" He looked at the body on the floor, clenching his fist repetitively.

"No." They took his arm, and started leading him away. "I disconnected his synthetics, somewhat crudely, but we should call for help."

He looked at the man on the ground, it was the one who'd broken his arm so easily before. Didn't seem so tough with the metal casing around his neck crushed, out cold from the shock. "No, his friends will. If they're any good."

They won't.

Ryoma let them pull him down the street and around the corner, feeling the bruises develop around his throat. The low level beat of music that played from every casino became more and more distant and distorted until it was a messy hum. Guin began chattering anxiously. "We should, we should go back, but what if I really hurt him? That..."

"They'd have killed us both otherwise, or me at least. You did good, ok?"

"Ok." They nodded, unconvinced and led him further down the street.

"Pacifist at heart aren't you?"

"I know I'm stronger than most, I just don't like to use it." They turned the corner in silence, the light in their eyes faded. Ryoma could see how heavily it weighed on them, he wondered if living so long was really a blessing after all, the build up of so much trauma over decades, centuries. Surely there was only so much one mind could take.

Guin's apartment was a lighthouse in the dark, the warm light spilling out from the open door. "I'll go first." They pressed their hand to his chest protectively.

The tiny apartment was upended, the furniture had been tossed and the windows smashed in.

"They must have just come from here," he said to no one in particular, following Guin into the upturned bedroom.

"We can't stay here, can we? Neither of us." They picked up a suit jacket from the floor, creased and trampled, feeling the weave of the fabric, speaking to it rather than him. "I'm sorry, I shouldn't have run. It's just when I saw myself there... I tried so hard to forget."

He touched their shoulder, bringing them out of their trance. "I'm the one that should be sorry, I've made this place dangerous for you."

"You didn't know all this would happen." They dropped the jacket to the ground and embraced him.

His mouth was dry, heart racing. "I had a visit a few days ago, from a corp enforcer, you know the sort. The corp must have caught wind of what I was looking into and told me to drop it."

They looked at him, face unreadable as the longest moment of his life passed. "Did you? Did you stop?"

"I thought I could, for you. To protect you. But when Sylph called, I couldn't say no. I just didn't realise it would be you."

"You should have told me Ryo. I'm not porcelain, I won't shatter." Their face was placid, he wondered if they could even be angry with him. He'd just seen the way they'd dispatched corp security, they were far stronger than he realised. They didn't need his protection, maybe they didn't need him at all. "I think it's you that needs help, Ryo."

He felt his heart begin to tear, things were falling apart all over again. "I thought if I kept you with me, they couldn't get you, but I just got you hurt anyway. I should have left you be. Pretty typical I would kick a hornet's nest just when I..."

Fall in love.

"Oh Ryo." Slowly, Guin leaned down and kissed his brow. "If it weren't for you, I'd still be here, singing every night, the same sets, the same crowd, I'd never have left probably. And I wouldn't have you either, how empty I would be." They picked up a piece of a broken window, rubbing their thumb along the broken edge, hard enough it would cut anyone else. "I'd still be lost, adrift."

He took their hand and squeezed just a little until they seemed to come to, dropping the piece of glass. They liked the people and noise, things he'd never appreciated, not really. There was that in abundance in the right places. "I think I know where we can go."

"You do?"

"The under-city, on Polaris. It's far deeper than I think even the corps realise, and there's the synth presence too. I think if we make contact, tell them what's happening, perhaps they'll take us in."

"I'll see if I can find my brother, if he'll take me. Won't they find us there? Raxle, Bio?"

"It's a maze down there, and corp security won't go in there most of the time. It's why I get so much work. It's where most people wash up in the system, we could search for others like you here, there may be others that remember. Maybe we can use that to strong arm them into leaving you alone, all of you."

"You think it can be done?"

"We have to try. It's what any halfway decent detective would do. Serena never stopped 'cause things got ugly, neither should I." He needed this, for her, and himself.

Ryoma's ear bud chirped softly, there weren't many people it could be. "Sylph?"

"Ryo, I wanted to apologise." She sounded worried. "I didn't realise till I saw them and the footage together, I - "

"We were followed, Syl." He cut in, increasingly aware that staying here was making them vulnerable. "I don't think it's safe here, for any of us. Have you got a fast way into Polaris? I think the Under is our best bet, disappear."

There was a lengthy pause on the line, to the point that Ryo thought the call had dropped. "Done. Make your way to the 'port asap, I'll get you where you need to go."

"Thank you Syl." He let out a breath.

Guin was already cramming clothes, and some loose sheets of paper into a small shoulder bag all whilst making clucking, cooing noises. "Perci? Perci, where are you?

A feeble mewling came from somewhere in the room, and a dusty orange cat crawled out from under the crushed bed. "There you are... I'm so sorry baby."

He rifled through the scattered ephemera around the apartment for any of his own affects. There was nothing that couldn't be replaced, just clothes and assorted junk, except for his new contact which he pocketed. Guin's gift. And Guin. Time to leave. "Darling, we need to go. Please, it's not safe."

"I know, I know. Let me grab her." Persimmon squeaked from under the bed, shaking off the dust. "She's old, I don't think she could cope with the travel. I'm sorry Perci, you have to stay here. I'll drop you with Aut, ok?" They scratched between her ears, brushing the dust away. " The cat looked at them blankly, headbutting their legs for more attention, and mewling as Guin scooped her into their arms. "Is a quick detour possible? I'll just drop her off, honest."

"Sure, if we're fast." He gave the apartment one last pass to check nothing identifiable was left behind.

"River, sweetie, I missed you!" Autumn's face brightened as the pair bundled into the Satellite, then dropped when he saw Ryoma's expression. "What's wrong?"

"We have to leave Aut, I'm so sorry."

Ryoma stood back to let them say their goodbyes, keeping his eye on the door and scanning for anyone inside who might be a threat. "I don't think we'll be back for a while."

"The two of you? Are you in trouble?" Aut's voice lowered, leaning across the bar so they could speak, and it fell below what Ryoma could hear. He checked the time on this wrist, still scratched and scuffed, and figured he'd give them a couple of minutes at least. He was already tearing them away from the sanctuary they'd found here, it was the least he could do. His throat still felt tight, he'd gotten so close to being killed again.

Just need to get home.

The door swung open suddenly, making Ryoma's stomach flip. In walked a pair of off duty door guards, already drunk it seemed, shoving past him as they went. A false alarm, but still they were cutting it too fine. There would be others coming after them soon enough. He leaned over and touched Guin's wrist. "We really gotta go darling, I'm sorry."

"He's right, you better run, little River."

"You're sweet, Aut. I want to ask you for a favour." They looked sadly at Persimmon, who had begun to wriggle uncomfortably in their arms. "Could you find somewhere for her? I'd be so grateful, I don't think she can travel at her age."

"I'd be honoured. I think she'll be right at home here," The cat wandered up the bar, sniffing customers' drinks and meowing at anyone who would listen. He leaned over the bar and hugged them tightly. "Be safe."

"Thank you." They smiled tightly, their eyes missing their usual sparkle. "Let's go Ryo."

Ryoma couldn't stop glancing behind him, sure they were still being followed. All the way to the 'port, every unfamiliar set of footsteps put him on edge. Guin clutched their bag tightly; occasionally checking the contents as they walked. From what he'd seen it was mainly a stack of their hand notated sheet music, their suit in dire need of pressing, and that borderline transparent dress they'd favoured on some nights.

A few streets before the port, his earbud trilled. "Ryo."

Sylph ushering them across to the cargo entrance. "These guys agreed to give you a lift straight to the Under."

"You're a miracle worker." He followed Sylph's lead through to the door. "I don't think I can thank you enough, Syl. Everything you've done when I've been such a horrible friend. I don't deserve you."

"Anything for Serena's bro, right?" Sylph slapped a hand on his shoulder as the little ship's cargo doors closed, winced a little at the name. He knew they'd been close, though he'd never asked just how close. "Just remember, you weren't the only one to lose her, you know."

"I've been a piece of shit, haven't I? For a while now."

"Everyone mourns different Ryo. I hope you two can find what you need."

He glanced back at Guin, hovering by the cargo bay door, anxiously waiting to board. "Me too."

Chapter Twenty

T he journey was short, restless. Ryoma couldn't sleep at all, lying on the too-small bunk and checking the time repeatedly and all the while Guin anxiously paced the room, pausing to look through the windows into the deep, shakily fidgeting with the buttons of their jumpsuit.

"Darling, you should try and rest."

"Says you," they stopped and sat by the tiny porthole. "I'm sorry I just, I wish I could go home, really go home. I wish you could have seen Hephaestus before it was scoured. It was so beautiful, especially the summer."

"I'm sorry." He sat opposite them, trying not to think too much about how aged the transport was, how the engine growled unhealthily. "We'll be ok, the under-city will be safe, the rentacop types they have on Polaris aren't going to want to search there. People will be willing to hide someone on the run from the corps. I know it's not the same, but I'll try and make it a home for you in the Under."

"You don't have to do all that." They smiled airily and stroked his cheek. He leaned into their touch, their cool hand a comfort against the sickly stale air of the ship. Guin pulled him closer, he felt himself begin to drift almost into sleep in their arms. He sat for a time, looking, unfocussed into the deep. The remains of his home could be out there, just dust now. Next to them lay one of Guin's sheets of music from their hastily packed bag. They had been reading them over and over for the last few hours to steady their frayed nerves. Crinkled and discoloured, the page could easily be much older than him. But Guin would look like that forever.

"You'll outlive me won't you?" He wondered aloud, watching the white points of starlight in the distance. "By a long, long, way."

"I suppose I will." He didn't see their reaction, but their voice sounded uneasy.

"What if I became like you?" He wondered what he'd look like with a body like theirs, no loss of strength, ageless, a body like glass... "Does it hurt?"

"The implant process? I'm not sure, I was mostly under when it happened. But I remember the first few months were quite an adjustment. Co-ordination, fine motor control, it all takes a few weeks to settle, it's like starting again. I had to relearn how to walk, speak, play the piano. That was the hardest part." Their voice hitched. "It's a lot to go through is what I mean. I can understand why people don't."

It must be hard to fall for someone like him and see them slip away. "It's not like I'm immortal, brain degradation is inevitable even with all the ways we can slow it. I'm still organic to a degree at the end of the day. But it'll be a long time, unless I'm badly hurt."

"You deserve a good long life darling. And hey, forty ain't dead, I've got a long time yet. If I go first, I'll wait for you," He smiled, kissing that spot along their jaw where the now imperceptible seam sat. It was hidden now, but he'd always know their secret. "I'll save you a good spot, I'm sure there's always space for an angel."

"Maybe I'll meet you there, when it's my time."

The ship landed on a private landing pad deep in Polaris Central, positioned on the rooftop of a steelglass vanity project that was largely unoccupied, since few people could afford the apartments there. Sylph pulled the pair of them aside and showed them on the screen that she had fudged the ship registration in the hopes it wouldn't be flagged by the corps. "This should give you an opening to get into the under-city, they won't be able to surveil you once you're there. Try to avoid the street cams."

"Where will you go?"

"Not far, I need to find a hangar that'll hide this thing." She turned to address Guin, squeezing their hand. "There are more of us than you think, Guin. Take care."

"Will she be ok?" They still held their bag in their arms the way they'd held their unruly cat, afraid it might escape.

"Sylph? She's had closer calls than this. She's tough."

Tougher than any of us.

"Come on, the further in we go, the less likely we are you'll be noticed. The Black Box was just on the outskirts." He took their hand and led them into the depths.

Guin's melancholy lifted as they walked around and the bare streets of the out began to populate again. "I...I recognise that person, they're from...they came here. And them too. I didn't realise there were so many of us still, I thought we'd all scattered."

Out of the crowd, someone approached them with his transparent hand over his chest in kind of greeting. Around his wrist was a serpent traced into the surface. Guin copied a beat or so later, remembering the half-forgotten custom. Ryoma had never seen anything like it. "Guin, it's been some time. I could hardly believe it when I heard you were coming. I thought you'd like to see your brother."

"Geo." He looked broadly similar to Guin in the face, the same flecks for hazel in their deep green eyes but his hair was short and choppy, his body broader than theirs. Guin threw their arms around him, holding him close. "It's been too long."

"It has, where have you been? I looked for you." Their almost-twin matched their embrace.

"I thought you'd have forgotten all about me."

"No, not you. The hive never forgets anyone it touches. Where were you Guin?"

"I've...been working, and I got lost, for a while. I just assumed you'd left for the deep or..." They trailed off guiltily, all this time they must have assumed they were all alone. "How did you know I was coming here?"

"There's been ripples, someone from 'phaestus thought they saw you and when I caught wind of a synth refugee arriving, in need of shelter ... I thought, I hoped, it might be you, and your new friend." The stranger's eyes darted to Ryoma, a smile on his lips.

"But..."

"But you didn't come back just to say hello, did you?"

They shrunk just slightly. "No, I'm afraid not. I, we, think someone's been targeting synths, for a while now too, including me."

"You heard of anything like it?" Ryoma, aware he'd been mystified by how similar they looked, felt like he should at least contribute.

The other synth regarded Ryoma properly for the first time, and nodded slowly. "There's been ripples, people showing up with memory loss, spinal damage, much like... There's not many, but enough to make people like us wary. We've been harbouring them here, the med-techs have been trying to recover what they can. A lot of them spend their time under the surface, but not many come back."

"Is there any way we can meet them? I want - I need to find someone else. Maybe we can stop this, make them leave us alone."

"Quite the detective you've become, little sibling." He lowered his voice, as a group of people walked past, their clothes screaming upper-city. "And I'm guessing whoever's doing this found you."

"We had a close call with some industry security off-world and we needed somewhere safe, all I could think of was here," Ryoma chipped in, not wanting to intrude on their reunion. "If you can't help me, just take in Guin. I'll take care of myself."

"If Guin trusts you, so do I, there'll always room for you here." Guin and Geo embraced again, this time touching a fingertip to their lip, then each touching the contact behind the other's ear.

"I'm sorry Geo, I should have come back sooner."

He pulled his hand away sharply, like he'd touched an open flame. The transference must be clearer between those with contacts. "No, no I am. If there's anything I can do sibling, just say the word. I'll help all I can."

They smiled and held his hands. "Thank you, and I'm glad you found people who make you happy."

"You'll have to come and meet them; I've told them all about you. Maybe you can bring Ryo."

"Of course, I'd, we'd love to." Guin turned back to Ryoma, who'd been overtaken with a powerful ache in his chest at the thought of being so easily invited into another family. "Are my rooms still open to me? We'd like to stay, if we can."

"Of course, there are no exiles, Guin. I asked that we leave them just as they were, all intact. The door will let you in as always. You tell me if you need help, ok?"

"I will, thank you." They ducked their head slightly in thanks, and took Ryoma's hand. There was a rumble overheard as another ship took off above them.

"You have a room?"

"A few of us grouped together and moved into a block. I had a little space of my own for a time, before I ran. But I think I remember the way at least. Come on, I'll show you." They walked down a side street, soft green lichen dampened their footsteps where it had crept through the concrete. Things weren't quite so sterile back here.

"You mentioned a family before, I didn't know he'd be so similar, I thought synths were all unique. I should have asked about him before."

I was being a self-involved jackass.

"It's alright, part of me thought I'd never see him again. Geo is my cluster brother. Our bodies are...were, made in batches and there's some level of duplication, little quirks here and there..."

"Like your eyes."

"Exactly. We were implanted at the same time at the old facility on Hephaestus, spent the recovery period together."

"Like a twin." It was more of a question than a statement, though they'd seemed very close.

"Yeah, a little like that, we've been close ever since. Well, we were. I haven't seen him since I left, never even called. I should have called."

"I'm sure you two can be close again." Guin stopped in front of a glass fronted building, dusting off a smooth panel next to the door and pressed their hand into its strangely soft surface.

"Do you know many others from your cluster family?"

They shook their head. "All the others were activated well before us from what I can tell, I think we were the last two. I've done a sweep before, most people with active clusters log their location regularly, or did last time I looked. A lot of us are crew on generation ships, heading out for the deep, so it could be a long time before I meet them. A lot of wanderers in cluster three seven oh."

"Just like you. You must miss them."

"I do, even if I've never met them. I wonder what they're like. Maybe they'll come back in a few decades, I'll just have to see where the astral wind takes them."

"It must be nice, knowing they're out there." The words came out more bitter than he meant to sound and he felt a guilty pang of jealousy in his gut.

"Yea- oh. Of course, I'm sorry. That was thoughtless."

"No, I'm being a jackass. It's good you've got people here darling."

"They're yours too, or they could be, if you stay." They kissed him, lips soft against his unshaven cheek. The doors slid silently open directly into a cosy living space. The furthest wall was entirely frosted glass. Guin tapped a few buttons on the wall and glass flickered, displaying a stormy ocean churned in the distance.

"There, much more homely," they said distantly. The heap next to the window was probably once a desk virtually buried under notebooks and loose sketches. "I can't believe he preserved it."

"This is really nice, cosy."

"You sound surprised," they hummed, unrolling a neatly bundled bed and shaking the creases in the sheets loose.

"I guess I was expecting something a little more... clinical, I suppose is the word? Your place on Scylla was pretty bare."

"I didn't take a lot with me when I left, and I lost quite a lot of what I took with me, I expected it all to be gone." They smiled weakly, looking at the messy desk. "I'm actually a bit of a hoarder. After Haephestus was taken over, I kept everything I could."

"I'm the opposite I think, I keep so little aside from a picture or two Serena made me save-" He cut himself off abruptly, and clenched his jaw. His memories of her were so twisted by their last minutes together, replacing all else with the animal terror he'd seen in her face. That photo was the reminder that Serena had been something other than that. Now locked in an apartment building crawling with BioMech lackeys, probably being bagged and burnt as they spoke. "I'm guessing those will be gone won't they? Shit."

"I'm sorry it came to this." Seeing his upset, they took his hand and gently led him to the window, the image sharpened as they approached to give the illusion of depth. There they were, stood on the precipice. "You wanted to see Hepaestus didn't you? Here, let me show you."

The pair gazed out of the window watching the storm, lighting struck the swirling oceans over and over. The curve of the small planet was just barely visible, and in the far distance he could just make out an enormous body thrashing about in the waves, a long flat tail coiling in the air as it dove back down to the deep. One of Guin's serpents, he thought. "It's just like you said."

"Isn't it just? It's one of the biggest storms recorded on Haephestus before we had to leave. One of my favourites." They tapped the glass and it became abruptly transparent, the ocean replaced with the bright community outside buzzing with activity. "Thank you for bringing me here, I've been so afraid to come back."

"As long as you feel safe."

They grinned. "I've got you Ryo. You said you'd keep me safe, I'm going to hold you to it." Considering how handily they'd knocked down Odette's lackeys, he was probably in more danger than they were.

"I'll try my best, darling."

Their gaze drifted down to street level. "We should find a pool."

"Pool?"

"To access the hive. I'd like to see if I can still dive after all this time."

"Sure, there's a couple around. Ain't been to any though, I couldn't tell you what's good."

"That's alright, we only need a hive feed, and maybe, if it works we can look for other victims. Geo said some of them spent all their time under."

Chapter Twenty One

The synaptic centre looked like a converted hotel to Ryoma's eye. Evenly spaced rooms, neutrally decorated and with the slight smell of cleaning solution. He even recognised it as they arrived. Sylph and Serena had badgered him to go for a dive but gave up asking after he had rain checked one too many times. He couldn't even remember why he'd refused, some childish belligerence that made him wary of new experiences until it was too late. Better late than never he supposed. Inside the room, there were a set of switches embedded into the floor next to his feet, cables leading from them to a small blank screen no bigger than a tablet.

Without a word, Guin crouched and keyed a code into the pad and several panels slid away, revealing a round pool around two metres across. It was empty but elaborately tiled in a tessellated pattern of oranges, purples, and reds, like a dual sunset. "Just like I remember. I thought all of this would be abandoned by now, that we were all scattered."

"This is nothing like those VR suites I've seen." Ryoma sat at the edge, running his hand along the cool smooth tile. "Anyone can use one of these, right?"

"Don't see why not - it's like one of those commercial tanks in holiday resorts, but you don't have a pre-programmed input, less structured."

"Those things always made me puke."

"They're a little rough on the senses."They fiddled with the controls on the poolside, and a viscous clear blue liquid began to pour in from an outlet in the corner. Guin watched it flow for a minute, mesmerised, and dipped a hand in to check the temperature. "Would you like to try? It's disconnected from the main hive for now so it'll just be us two."

"Just us two. Is it safe, for someone like me?" He watched the gel as it poured into the pool, rippled reaching out to the edges and bouncing back with diminishing returns. "I don't have anything like you."

"Sure. I mean if anything it should be safer, since the connection isn't as strong, you can only go so deep without these things." They tapped one of the silver strips behind their ear. "And I'll be there too, to ground you if you need a quick exit."

Ryoma watched the tiled pattern shift and glow invitingly, and dipped his hand in to let it flow between his fingers, making ripples of his own. He was so drawn in that he barely noticed the rustle of clothes behind him. A strategic cough snapped him out of his trance and he looked up; Guin had stripped down to short leggings that clung low on the waist in a way that made his mouth water. "You look...really good?"

"You like it?" They crouched and draped their arms around his shoulders. "I thought you might."

"I do, darling." He mouthed at their neck, feeling himself get distracted. He needed to stay on track for once, for them. "Shit sorry, what were you saying?"

"The gel helps all the thoughts and feelings flow, you won't get the full effect without the contact seams but..." They trailed off, noticing his slightly bewildered look, the idea of his mind being laid bare hadn't occurred to him, and they could see it. "You don't seem too sure about this..."

"Will you see everything?" He asked, trying to refocus on the pool before him. It seemed deeper than it was just a minute ago. There was a lurching feeling in his gut that everything, every errant stray thought, every impulse, would just slip out before he could stop himself.

"Are you getting shy on me, Ryo?" They teased, letting their fingers trail in the liquid. "It won't be everything, not if you don't want to. Although strong feelings can affect how it feels, what manifests when you're in here."

Manifests?

His mind raced with the possibilities both painful and embarrassing, there was so much he instructually didn't want them to see. But they'd been so open with him, trusted him with a lot they'd kept secret for so long. He swallowed hard and pushed the feeling aside as best he could, he'd have to trust them sometime.

"Some people do get a kind of motion sickness, but we'll go slow, you can gauge how you feel." They handed him two small devices, like coin sized silver beetles. "Here, just put these in, like your earbuds. They'll help you stay balanced and make the connection much clearer, even without implants."

"And, if we just..." they continued, taking his silence as understanding and letting their feet slip into the gel. He stripped to his underwear and followed suit, sitting next to them on the edge. It was thicker and colder than he expected and tinged ever so slightly blue, washing out the warmth from his skin tone. The new buds made his hearing feel occluded and isolated, so he looked at Guin expectantly, waiting for what would happen next. He was about to speak when suddenly he felt a strange shiver, a flash of warmth and euphoria from within. He sat up trying to identify the feeling, familiar but alien, like it belonged to someone else.

"You feel it, don't you?" Guin's voice was low, reverent.

"It's..." He felt a lightness in his chest, and a smile, uncontainable, reached his lips.

"It's me. Well, just a little of me. Of how I feel." They bit their lip and swung their feet in the gel, slowed by the viscosity. "I can feel you too."

"Never felt anything like it, it's beautiful." Their fingers interlaced, shifting a little closer to each other.

"That's just a little taste," Their voice shifted, sounding like a rippling echo inside his own head, clearer than anything he'd ever heard before. "Is it alright?"

"Yeah, is there more?" Ryoma's vision began to twist, his surroundings seemed to shift and distort. He held their hand tighter, trying to center himself. "What's happening?"

"You're connecting to the hive. Or at least a small part of it. It can be disorienting until you get used to it. You'll see." Guin slid into the pool quickly, the gel barely rippling around their waist, for him it was a little deeper. They put a hand on his shoulder and another on his hip, guiding him onto his back.

"Just let yourself lie back and sink, it's oxygenated so don't worry about breathing. Try to relax into it."

"Can't keep your hands off me, can you?"

They smiled as he lay back and began to sink, trying to overcome the survival instinct that compelled him to sit and splutter ungracefully. He had to trust that Guin knew what they were talking about, and relax as the strangely warm gel filled his lungs. His throat tried to reflexively reject it for a few seconds, until his mind overcame the animal instinct that he was drowning. Gravity did the rest, and he sank down just short of the tiled floor and hung there suspended, weightless. The pressure fluctuated as Guin joined him a foot or so away, a muted splash. They brushed their fingers against his as they settled. For his comfort or theirs, he couldn't tell. Maybe both. Above him the ceiling began to whirl and liquify, the features of the room slid away into a wash of unfocussed colour and noise as he began to drift.

Further and further down into the synaptic ocean he sank, Guin's hand in his, until his senses began to stabilise. Under his feet he felt soft, loose sand shift, his clothes were back and less crumpled than usual. Even in his wildest imagination he wore mostly black, apart from the jacket, the faded pilots jacket he'd pilfered from his sister. It was quiet here, just the white noise of the beach, and grey sand shifting with each step. In the distance the tiny figure of Guin waved, ushering him over. Their casing was gone, leaving just their face plate and their hair pushed back.

"You like the beach, I thought it might be more comfortable for you, tangible. Some people try to experience something abstract and impossible right away and it scrambles their brains." They watched him take a few unsteady steps towards the shore. Out to sea one of the serpents thrashed amongst the waves, a great red and black tail, flattened at the end and striped, crashed onto the surface before disappearing. "There's a little bit of my home too. "

They didn't seem to be speaking visibly but he heard it just as well.

"This is what I wanted to show you earlier, what I tried to show you, before all of this."

"The beach works, I'm a bit of a sun worshipper. But you knew that." Ryoma was surprised to find his lips didn't move either. He couldn't quite believe this place, it was so familiar and yet, not quite. "This isn't like any VR suite."

"Oh, it's much more than that." The soft light caught the hazel flecks in their left eye, and their faltering smile. "It's been a long time, too long. I felt disgraced, I suppose, after what happened. Like I'd poison it with my presence." He could feel it too, their shame, emotions seemed to flow more easily between them than words. But there was a brightness there too, their heart open to his own.

"This is how I remember Polaris, not too long before you were born I imagine." Instinctively, Ryoma looked around for anything familiar, a landmark, the city. "Geo used to bring me here all the time, before I left."

Guin stood mystified at the horizon, unmoving for so long he thought they'd disconnected, glitched out. He remembered how they'd looked with such longing at the murky Polaris sea before. "How about a swim? I'm assuming nothing can get us sick in here."

Their face lit up. "Race you to the shore."

He made to run but Guin was far ahead suddenly, transported into the surf in a blink, and disappeared under.

Ryoma ducked under the water to follow, and instinctively held his breath for a second before he remembered where they were, and relaxed. He did his best to track them, their transparent body blended into the sea so much they could have been part of it. Only the flickering lights inside them and the dark sway of their hair guided his way. Without physical limits he swam further and deeper than he'd ever done before, until he found Guin waiting for him, kneeling on the seabed. Even down here the far-reaching sun light revealed their smile, drawing him in. He reached out to touch when they suddenly propelled themself away, grey sand churned in their wake as they swam around him and kicked up and away.

Ryoma surfaced too, looking around the vast blue surf for Guin, when he felt a ripple around his legs, then a touch brushing his ankle and a tug at his shorts, though he didn't remember changing. "Hey!"

Guin slid behind him squeezing his shoulders and kissed his throat, wet and warm. The serpent on their chest softly illuminated the water around them, pulsing slowly. "You're a natural, a mermaid or something. Or one of these critters I imagine."

"I was born to it, could swim before I could walk. That said, I'm not really swimming right now am I?" How easy it was to forget. They tangled legs with his, a hand squeezing his soft stomach, sliding under his waistband. "Am I touching you right now?"

He felt himself gasp. Could he gasp in here? "Feels just as real to me, darling."

They smiled. "It'll feel a little strange here, a little intense."

"Is that a no?" He paused, wondering if he'd crossed some kind of boundary, a custom unheard of. They pressed their lips to his in response, allowing him to guide them down to the sand. Something around them began to shift again, flesh and metal and glass became fluid. The boundaries between their bodies seemed to blur, fade into each other.

He pulled back, the ghost of the sensation on his lips. "That's ...different. Is it always like that?"

"Even better. Like this you can share a lot more, feel a lot more." Their voice was inside his head again, like a soft whisper that tickled his neck.

They withdrew their hand and looked back to the shore. "We should take this slow. I don't want to overwhelm you."

"Course." He couldn't help but be a little disappointed after getting a taste of this place, their touch, had left him craving more.

Guin took his hand and suddenly he was back on dry land, so to speak, in a mere blink. Impressed with their mastery, he sat in the sand and rifled through the jeans he didn't remember putting on and found a fresh pack of cigarettes and a lighter he was sure he'd lost years ago. It had a familiar, homely click as it ignited and on that first inhale he felt like he was home, pilfering it from his mother's room to smoke the ashy floor sweepings that the traders at the port called cigarettes. She only used it to light candles when the electricity was on the fritz, their childhood home given a warm orange glow against the cold dark, the four of them watching some show on their tablet until the battery ran dry.

"I've missed that sound, there's nothing like it." Guin shut their eyes, their face serene as they listened to the hushed whisper of the sea.

"Hm." Ryoma lay back in the sand looking up at the distant unfamiliar constellations, not that he could read a star chart for the life of him anyway. "Helps me think, when I'm stuck on a case. Or I needed to wind down after a fight. I always used to listen to the rain as a kid, still do. Hey can we -"

He opened his eyes to look at Guin but they were gone, the beach empty for miles in either direction. He called out to them, to no response, hoping they were just teasing him like before. But minutes passed, maybe, there was no way of telling, Guin was nowhere to be found. Ryoma began to walk, he wasn't sure what direction, the cliff face had disappeared when he wasn't looking, grey sand in all directions, the sound of waves persistent but no water to be found. He wondered if they could have disconnected somehow, a crueller part of him wondered if they'd left him there and when he surfaced they would have left him.

Wait.

How do I leave? How do I...

He'd tried basic VR before, nothing this immersive, but still he tried to remember the emergency exit strategies he'd used when his inner ear rejected the simulation. Applying pressure on the wrists, tapping twice on the temple, nothing. He kept on moving, hoping to find the edges, only for the horizon to remain in place. Panic began to grip him and almost like it sensed this, the landscape changed too, became unstable and twisting.

I need to get out.

The mutating space made his stomach lurch, he tried to focus on the forming horizon to steady himself but the light of the suns became unbearable, the bright colours of the sea merged into a sickening slurry and the once subtle waves became louder and louder like a rushing waterfall, unbearable static. He felt the ground beneath him crack, a tunnel collapse would take him like it had his parents. He'd seen Guin's nightmare, could they see his? The sand under him began to fall away and he started to sink, losing traction on falling through the floor, through the ground, deeper and deeper. Too deep, too fast.

The air was thick and syrupy, his lungs full of fluid, his body shuddering, choking with panic. He shut his eyes trying to focus like Guin had said, when the sound stopped, replaced with a sickly all too familiar gasping.

No.

"Serena?" She was slumped against a half-formed wall that seemed to be phasing in and out, half-rendered flickering like a degraded recording. He crouched trying to see through the edge of the simulation. "Why are you showing me this?"

"Ryo," She didn't seem to hear him, her voice was thin and her eyes watery and wide. Even the faded green of her hair was as he remembered. "Where are you?"

"I...I'll get you help sis, I..." He tried to stand but she grasped on to his jacket, smearing red down the sleeve as she pulled him back down. Her eyes filled with the terror of someone who knows they're too far gone. The jacket would never clean. He'd throw it away after scrubbing it into oblivion, unable to remove his sister's blood from it. "I, I can do things right this time."

"I'm scared Ryo."

"I know, just, try not to move." He pressed his hand to the ragged tear on her stomach, but seemed to sink sickeningly inward, hot blood oozing through his fingers. "Oh fuck, I'm... I really need to get you help, I can't lose you too..."

"Ryo, don't, don't go." She grasped at him tightly pulling his wrist, even speaking was exhausting for her. He'd forgotten just how similar she looked to him even after half a lifetime change.

"But I need to get - " He tried to insist, even though no one would take them in.

"Please." Serena's voice was a faint sigh, weaker than he'd ever heard before.

"It's ok, ok, I'm right here." He tried to keep pressure where he could, his chest pounding so hard he felt sick, his steel hand the only steady part of his body. "I'm here, See? I'll stay...I'll stay here."

Do you remember the rain?

"Ryo?" A new voice called, he looked around for the source of the sound but then his sister was gone, his hands trembling where she'd been before. Still soaked.

"She was right here..."

"Ryo, Ryo it's me. Just hold on, try to breathe steady." He couldn't see anyone, but he felt the pressure of a hand squeezing his shoulder, strong and cold, lifting him to his feet. Guin. "Just focus on my voice, ok?"

His vision went briefly white and he was suddenly back in the pool, the grey industrial fan above them, the screen on the wall that controlled the temperature. He resurfaced, spluttering gel from his lungs, his throat and eyes raw.

"What the fuck was that?" Ryoma spat, more sharply than he meant to. He tried to lift himself out of the pool, but his strength was gone. He'd left her behind. "Why was..."

Why was she there?

He looked up at Guin, who was already sitting on the edge of the pool, their jaw tight, holding out their hand for him to take.

"You sank Ryo, fast and deep. I almost lost you." They helped him climb out, taking his weight as easily as ever, then pulling away to close the cover.

"Didn't realise it could feel so real." His eyes stung at the memory of her voice, his twin reduced to another body on the street. Serena's voice had been so clear, like a recording. Ryoma spread his hands on the floor, glad to be on solid ground again and with each shaking breath, his terror began to slip away like just another half-forgotten nightmare.

"It was her, wasn't it?"

"She was right there..." He blinked hard, clenching his fists. "I couldn't do anything, I couldn't..."

"I had no idea it was so - I'm so sorry Ryo." Guin knelt next to him, passing him a towel but avoiding his eye when he tried to meet them.

He dried off and checked his wrist; the lack of windows in the room enhanced the disconnection to reality. Somehow, it was very early morning, local time. They'd lost most of the day. "It's been hours, what - what the fuck happened?"

"Time falls away so fast in there, it's - "

"Fluid." Ryoma could have spent years in there and never known, it was no wonder people got lost. All those people he'd pulled out of VR suites screaming to be put back in. He let out a ragged breath, a breath he'd been holding in for four years. She was really gone. "A liquid thing."

"I just wanted to show you everything, for it to be perfect. I never thought - "

They looked at him despondent from behind the sweep of their hair, placing their hand next to his, crystal reflecting in the pale light of the room. He took their hand, pressing it to his chest. Guin's cool skin was a balm to his overworked nervous system, calming his racing heart. "I ain't a goner just yet darling, and neither are you."

The pool room was so gloomy, so saturated with the smell of cleaning fluid, that he began to feel the walls looming over them, too close. He needed air.

"Let's get a little suns-light."

Chapter Twenty Two

Ravenously hungry from the dive, Ryoma took Guin to the community kitchen nearby. He took an embarrassing amount of food from the kiosk; bread, bao, buns, anything starchy and guiltily stuffed a fist full of crumpled notes in the collection box, bypassing the reader on his wrist. Scanners would be no good if they wanted to stay off the radar. Guin brought a pot of coffee to the table and picked slowly at a small slice of something cake-adjacent. Between sips, they would look up to take a fleeting glance at Ryoma as he ate, timidly checking in on him. They had this look like a frightened animal.

"You know, I'd have thought synths would skip eating altogether," he said, breaking the silence as he was chasing the last few scraps around the bowl. "Seeing as you hardly need it."

"What exactly were you imagining I'd eat?" Their expression broke into a confused smile, pouring a little more coffee for themself. A torrential downpour outside had emptied the street, forcing a few more people inside for cover filling the few tables around them, unwrapping their more delicate synthetics and bringing with them the clammy humidity of drying coats and boots.

"I don't know, like nutrient paste? Something very functional I guess." He felt ridiculous even as he said it, but it took

"So, soylent green? Grey goo?" They smirked into their drink.

"Huh?"

"I'm sure there are some that do but it's one of life's pleasures, amongst other things." Their bare ankle slid against his; "I can't think of many people that would forsake that, would you?"

He shook his head.

"This is a hint I want you to cook for me again by the way."

Ryoma smiled weakly. His mood dragged downward by the after effects of the pool. He clenched his fists again, trying to shake the memory loose.

Guin shifted in their seat. "I'm sorry about what happened Ryo."

"It's alright, it was just unexpected is all." He shrugged, fiddling with a crushed empty cigarette pack he'd found in his jeans. Guin didn't look convinced, watching him with the expression of someone who's lived long enough to know better. "It's just, that's not how I wanted to remember her. She was hurt and afraid and I was just useless. We had corp enforcers on our tail, like we do now. I was supposed to have her back but, I was too slow, I just fucked it all up."

Guin leaned across the table and took his synthetic hand to calm it. He hadn't even noticed he'd been tapping the surface quite so much until he stopped, the tabletop still ringing. "You were with her?"

"I was...it just happened so fast."

Their hand squeezed his. "You stayed with her. It's not much but, I'm sure she was glad to be with you, before the end. I know I'd hate to be alone."

"Yeah." He didn't mention all the nights he wished he'd gone with her, or in her place. He squeezed their hand, soft and transparent in his, the mechanical insides glittering. They seemed so delicate, he still couldn't believe what he'd seen before. "I should, should really get back to work. I need to finish this. I need to get enough leverage to get these guys off your back."

"But what about you Ryo?"

I don't care what happens to me.

But he couldn't say that. His feelings were muddying the water, he had to think methodically, despite everything. "You're the witness darling and I ain't the priority. What we need is to find others like you, who've been hurt the way you have."

They nodded. "I was thinking, if we connect to the hive properly, I might be able to find others who were attacked. Those records, my own memories, it could jog someone else's. If nothing else, maybe people knowing will be enough to stop it from happening."

He smiled grimly at the thought of going back. "Are you sure it won't be too much for you after what happened? Guin, darling..."

"Says you!" They said with a dry laugh, louder than they had meant to. They gripped onto their cup, looking around the canteen at the other patrons and lowered their voice. "I have to try, don't I? If they can hurt me, they can hurt all of us. And if they get what they want, they'll just cement themselves deeper and deeper, until there's nothing left and we can't even breathe without them. I've been gone for so long I have to do something. Please, let me help. You don't have to do everything yourself."

"I just don't want you getting hurt. They've already done so much to you."

"They can't hurt me more than they already have. I'm more worried about you. You can't do a deep dive on a public network on your second try, not after how your first went. That's a lot for anyone to take."

"I know." He let out a shaky breath. They were right of course; he was terrified to go back. The feeling of sinking, never drowning but slipping out of reach, trapped at the bottom of the ocean with no one but a ghost but for company. He needed them. "Ok."

"Thank you. I'll need to get reacquainted with the network and it might take me a couple hours to reset the pool's connection to the hive. How about you go for a walk around, stretch your legs and getting some face time between dives can help ground you." Guin's face set into a stolid expression he'd never seen before and he believed that they really could stop this. They pressed their lips to his, as urgent and wanting as they had been the first time. "I'll see you soon, Ryoma."

"Guin."

I love you.

Slowly the rain subsided enough for Ryoma to leave the kitchen and out into the warm spring air that flowed between the tightly packed buildings, quickly drying the ground under his feet. Ryoma passed by a bar that he was sure sounded familiar when he felt a tap on the shoulder.

"Sere- oh." He turned, half expecting a fight, but instead stood a woman with cropped, faded blue hair looking at him wide-eyed, cigarette hanging from her lips. "Shit, I'm sorry I thought you were someone else."

She was about to turn away into the bar, when he caught her elbow noticing her halfway rusted set of hands.

"No, wait. Serena LeBeau?" The woman nodded, briefly looking back into the bar with hands on hips. "I'm her brother."

"Of course, the famous twin! I was so sure I'd seen a ghost. Come in, come in! I run this place." She pinched the half smoked cigarette out with half way rusted finger and thumb and tucked it into the breast pocket of her shirt. He followed her inside and perched at the bar as she hopped over it. Embedded into the wall was a cracked screen with a mess of cables and attachments clung to it. "So, you're the boxer brother huh?"

"Not anymore, but yeah. I'm Ryo."

"Yeah that's right, knew it was something like that. I'm Lana. Man, she'd always talk about you. Haven't seen her around these parts in years, figured the business took off, until I heard what happened." She bit her lip. "Bad business that."

"Not been the same without her."

"Serena saw every one of your fights, used to come down here to watch."

"She did?"

"Her friend came by one day, hooked up a split feed into the bar. She used to look so anxious every time you took a punch, but you always got right back up." Lana cocked a pierced eyebrow. "You never knew?"

"She never told me." He'd always known the fights were streamed, but he'd never gone out of his way to watch them, unable to stand looking at himself at the time. But he'd never even thought Serena would be watching, she made such a show of hating it.

"Siblings, huh?" She hopped behind the bar and ducked down. He looked around the cramped ramshackle bar with the walls, a patchwork of photographs, layers and layers of people that had passed through over the years. Ryoma let his eye pass over the multitude of strangers for anyone he knew even in passing and then there she was. The familiar face of his sister grinning in that wide, uninhibited way she did after a few drinks, holding onto Sylph's shoulder. Her hair was a vibrant, metallic purple, she must have just dyed it at the time. The muted sound of a fridge closing caught his attention as a bottle of Belter's hissed open. Lana smiled. "On the house, for her."

"For her," he said faintly and took a long drink.

Chapter Twenty Three

Ryoma returned to the centre with some groceries in hand, mainly self-heating coffee and anything shelf stable he could get his hands on, knowing he'd be starving after another dive. A half asleep desk clerk pointed in the direction of the room without checking his ID, so let himself in. Ryoma kicked off his boots at the door and sat at the edge of the pool for what felt like hours, watching Guin as they lay nude and suspended in the pool, eyes shut but twitching subtly as though they were dreaming. They looked peaceful, at home, in there.

Why couldn't he feel that?

His hands jittered with anxiety, or maybe withdrawal. In his daze, he'd not bought any cigarettes and popping a stim just before connecting his brain directly to the hive seemed like a recipe for a crash. With little fanfare, Guin's eyes flickered open and they pushed themself up silently to the surface, elbows resting on the tiled edge of the pool. They pushed their hair back and gazed up at him with a lazy smile. More than ever they seemed like a mermaid, a siren, waiting to draw him into the ocean. They had the voice for it. "You could have woke me up early."

"Not a chance." Ryoma bit his lip looking down at them slick with synapse gel.

"You like to watch me, don't you?" They moved closer, taking his hand, kissing each of his scuffed steel knuckles. "It's alright Ryo, I like it. When you watch me sing, or dive, or ride you."

Ryoma's breath felt heavy. "Yeah, I do."

"But we should get on shouldn't we? I'm sure we can find time afterwards." They let go of his hand, waving towards the flickering wall screen "It's all reconnected, so we can dive when you're ready."

"We?"

"I was thinking I could be your guide, show you the way. It can be somewhat labyrinthine, if you're not born to it. I'm a little rusty but the hive remembers everyone it touches. It'll come back to me." They smiled, soft and lilting. "Did you really think I'd come all this way and not help you?"

"Of course not." He shrugged and started to undress. "Seems like you're my guardian angel after all. It'd be bad luck *not* to take you at this point."

"Then we better not jinx it." They grinned, their eyes sparkling in the light and passed him the earbuds from before. He put them in and sat himself at the edge of the pool, trying to will himself into the pool. It would be different this time. It had to be. Guin tapped at a tablet plugged into the wall outlet. "This should capture anything we find, that way it's all recorded right?"

"You really are quite the detective, Guin."

"I don't know about that Ryo, I just think of what you'd do." They watched keenly as he finished undressing and slid further into the pool inviting him to follow. He followed shortly after, dunking under the surface for a second to push his hair back.

Immediately things began to shift as the contacts connected to the gel, even for a brief second. Sound and colour distorted where he'd stood so quickly. There was a lot more noise too, like static that needed tuning out.

"Just relax and let yourself sink just like before, ok?" Their voice was quiet, almost reverent. Ryoma felt the weight of his body lift away and his vision began to warp again, but slower this time, more languid. As he slipped under he felt the gentle cool touch of a hand on his. Theirs. "I'm right here, remember."

The world fell away and they sank further and further down, until they reached a floor of sorts and the light returned to his eyes. He looked around where they had been dropped into the open hive, shadows of other users passed through and over him, an innumerable amount of paths twisting away in every direction. People walked above and below them on invisible layers, with seemingly way to get up or down. Guin appeared on his right, their projected self fully dressed, back in those silver shoes of theirs. "What do you think?"

"This is incredible, but I think we might have to save the tour for later."

"Of course, I put out some inquiries like you said." They waved their hand in the air and pulled a tablet out of nothing, showing him. "I wasn't really sure what to say, so I just told them what happened to me. Nothing too detailed but, the gist."

"Any bites?"

They gave him an unreadable expression for a moment. "A few, more than I thought actually. And they want to talk." Guin took his hand and led him on.

As they approached the ground became more unstable, swelling and pulsing as though it were alive. The ground heaved itself into a solid shape, a dome of opaque crystal or glass. The crystal dome flowed apart to create an entrance for them. "What is it?"

"I've never seen anything like it." Guin laced their fingers with his as they tried to make sense of it all. "It's way more complex than before, this is far beyond me."

"Are you responding to our message?" Ryo called to the space around them, the coloured crystal walls rotating through blues and greens. Before him, a crowd of bodies appeared, a few dozen at least, pale shapes, surrounding the two of them closely. Not threatening but curious, mostly humanoid shape, some less so.

"You know this?" Guin let go of his wrist, turning to show their scar. There were murmurs of recognition from the ghostly bodies.

"We know it." Their avatars were deidentified shadows, speaking together in a flat toneless voice. "All of us."

"How many of you are here?"

"Over thirty here, many more left the system for the deep, others are gone entirely."

"Gone." They replied, then spoke up. "Are you all hardwired?"

"Wired?" Ryoma was out of his depth.

"Their brains are permanently submerged. No bodies."

"Many of us are." Ryoma could see what Guin had meant by people getting lost. They don't want bodies and who could blame them for ridding themselves of what made them vulnerable.

Wait.

"Guin what if it was their bodies? Could there be a weakness, something to exploit?" They looked at him questioningly, the pieces beginning to click between them. "Ask for their specs. There has to be something, they wouldn't have been able to scrape just anyone and everyone, BioMech and Raxle were looking for something specific. A particular build or model, something."

They nodded. "We just have one thing to ask of you if you would. Could you send through your readouts of your bodies, the ones you had when it happened? If we can find what makes us targets we can stop it, cut them off, maybe." The space fell silent and the avatars abruptly evaporated. "Please."

"Will it work?" He said, remembering too late he didn't need to speak in here.

"I don't know, I've never seen anything like this." Guin's voice sunk back into his head and they both waited as an internal discussion between the group ensued, muted voices overlapping in unclear debate. "We'll have to wait."

Ryoma knelt down and touched the solid crystal floor, trying to make sense of the disconnect - the reality that he was submerged in a glorified paddling pool. He tried to remember the liquid surrounding him, his hand slowed by its viscosity, but here he couldn't feel anything.

"I don't think we can influence what happens here, not as individuals."

"Probably for the best," Ryoma scoffed. "I don't think we want to inflict the content of my head on anyone. You think they made this thing?"

"If they're hooked in permanently, they've had time. Protecting themselves the only way they know how." The walls curved up and away, colours fluctuating through emerald and turquoise shades, ink dropped into water. "Like I did. We both did."

They joined him on the ground, kneeling and running a finger along the hairline cracks in the crystal with a gentle familiarity. It could have been minutes or hours by Ryoma's count, watching the ceiling above pulse and shift hypnotically, trying to think of a backup if this didn't work. The corps wouldn't stay out of this part of the city forever unless he found some way to repel them, and he couldn't leave other synths to this fate. Not after what Guin had suffered.

No, this had to work. If they were after him, he was moving in the right direction.

The muffled speech subsided abruptly, drawing Ryoma and Guin's attention through their silence. "We have agreed to give you what you need, some of us will give our original schematics."

It wasn't much but,

"Thank you, thank you all." Guin put their hand to their chest, Ryoma did the same after a beat and the room suddenly fell away into nothingness, spitting them back into realspace. The sudden drop made Ryoma's stomach lurch, hurling him back into their room with a splash and a splutter. He groaned, climbing stiffly out of the pool and collapsed on the floor, his body feeling impossibly heavy after the weightlessness of the pool.

"Does it always wipe you out like that?"

"You get used to it, it's just harder on organics." They glanced at him with a smile, perched on the edge of the pool, gazing in. They ran their fingers along the knotted scar tissue on their neck, deep in thought. "There were so many like me. The company must have been trying for so long."

"Yeah, there were." He sighed, feeling guilty for acting so blasé. "I'm sorry darling."

The tablet chirped as the readings from the others arrived. Still dripping, the two huddled around it and began to examine them for any similarities. Some of them had only released partial specs, hidden some key aspects of themselves but it was enough to compare with Guin and who could blame them after what happened. Most were much much older than them, a few younger, some humanoid, some more functional or fantastical in design. But they *had* all lived on Hephaestus, received maintenance and upgrades from their original bodies, except for...

Ryoma clucked his tongue. *There it was.*

"These people, they've all got BioMech shells, the original brain casing? All refitted to some degree but they can't remove it all, right?" He remembered the recent output from Guin's maintenance cycle. It hadn't made sense to him at the time, but it was so similar. "These readings on the brainwork, it's like you showed me, right?"

Guin flicked through a couple of screens, scrolling through reams of data faster than he could process. "Oh God - you're right. They're all like me Ryo, they're all refits. Someone like BioMech probably told them they could brute force their way in, scrape the schematics out."

They laughed bitterly in a strange, strangled noise that made Ryoma uneasy, leaning

"What is it?"

"Fucking foolish. We'd have given it away, if they asked, if they'd been reasonable. But they never thought to, or maybe they didn't want to."

"A company like BioMechanics won't admit they can't do something." They'd outsourced it.

They stared vacantly into the pool for some time, leaning forwards so far he thought they might fall right in. "That's the way of things isn't it."

"It doesn't have to be." He held their cheek, and leaned in for a kiss, slow and deep, fingers brushing the cool strip behind their ear.

I love you. The thought passed through him so quickly but he knew it was true. Guin's kiss deepened too.

I love you too, Ryo. The unexpected reply made him jolt back.

"You heard that?" He touched his jaw to be sure he'd truly spoken, his voice feeling alien to his ear. They'd never discussed what they had, it just felt natural. He'd never thought to say the words, that they might be too delicate to survive him speaking them.

"Your feelings come through so strongly, I thought you meant to." They held his hand still slick with the gel, rubbing circles on his palm. The ink on their chest softly illuminated them both with pale blue light. "You've got such a distinct feel to you, unique."

"I didn't realise I was that easy to read." He felt almost embarrassed that he'd been so obvious.

"It's nothing to be ashamed of, wearing your heart on your sleeve. You've always felt very open with me, even if I haven't."

Is that how they always seemed to know what he'd like? He remembered their reunion with their brother, passing their memories through to each other with touch. He sat up suddenly with the realisation their brother could have seen them together. "Have you been able to read me before?"

"Not clearly without the gel, just feelings that wash over when you touch me, mostly when we're in bed." They glanced downward with a smirk. "I could feel how worked up you were, what worked, what didn't."

"Huh, so that's how you knew. Here I was thinking you could have been made for me." He scoffed, feigning disappointment.

"Maybe I was." They leaned in and kissed along his throat. "And you for me."

The pool began to drain of its own accord, breaking the quietness of the moment, and the lights in the room became uncomfortably bright, revealing the tired hotel interior of the room.

Their time was up.

Ryoma began to dress, realising these were all he had since his own rooms were a no-go. "We should go back to your place, figure out what to do with all this."

Guin remained unmoved for a few long moments - staring at the tablet so hard, so unblinkingly, he thought it might crack from their sheer will. With everything else they were capable of; he wouldn't have been surprised. "This is probably a little more than you're used to huh?"

"It is, but we'll get this out there, I promise." He pulled on his jacket and tucked the tablet into his pocket.

Guin nodded slowly and began to pull their clothes on, the loose jumpsuit's length hiding the transparency of their body.

"You wanted me to cook for you again didn't you?"

Back at the apartment, Ryoma could feel Guin hovering closely behind him as he cooked, observing the process for posterity. The space Guin had for food preparation was so small it could hardly be called a kitchen at all, but if he was careful there was just enough to put together a batch of the dumplings they'd been so interested in before. "Sorry, I'm being strange aren't I."

"Not at all, darling. Would you like to help?" He pressed the edges of the dumpling together, the ridges of his segmented metal fingers leaving a distinct texture. He added it to the row he'd already made and indicated to Guin. "Now you try."

He stood behind them, his hands over theirs, not that they needed it. They dexterously scooped up just the right amount of filling and exactly replicated the pleats. "Like this?"

"Perfect. You can keep going if you want." He pressed his nose into their hair, soft and lightly perfumed, pressing against the curve of their back. He'd almost forgotten what it was like to slow down, or cook for someone else. "You know, no matter how messy things get, making a few rows of these, everything goes quiet for a few minutes. Straightens everything out."

Guin hummed softly as they assembled the rest of the dumplings and heated the pan. It was the melody of the song they'd written for him. Ryoma pressed against them tighter in the hope they could fill the ache in his heart. "I love you, Guin."

"I love you too." Guin touched their flour-dusted hand to his own, interlacing their fingers as the dumplings began to crackle under the heat.

When the food was ready, they sat by the window and ate quietly, the screen switched off so they could watch the constant flow of people outside. So many were living outside the influence of the corps, more than he thought. Maybe it was possible to live without them.

"So what now? We've got to make this public somehow." They asked, pushing the remaining food toward Ryo.

"If you can get them out on the news feed, maybe enough people will see before the corp forces them to pull the story. We'll need a source on the inside though, something to prove it. I don't want to release that footage of, of you. And besides, they'll say the surveillance was faked, that you're lying. Deny, deflect... whatever the rest of that saying is."

"So we'll need a whistleblower?"

"Something like that, someone from inside at least. Maybe we can get Rearden to talk, this whole mess took a lot from him."

"Where is he now?" Guin stacked the empty bowls, adjusting them so one sat exactly within the other. "You saw him here, right? On Polaris?"

Rearden had seemed like someone who was a little lost, in need of distraction. And the Under was good for that. "Yeah, and I think I know where he'd be."

Chapter Twenty Four

The Wonderland VR suites had been state of the art maybe a decade ago, but when the glamour faded and the novelty wore off the owners started to run a far more specialist service. Illicit programs, memory data stolen through jacking or sold by people who needed the credits, all configured to the sensory inputs. Ryoma had been there before on business and it was as grotesque as he remembered, the crimson coloured lights kept low to disguise the customers from each other. As they walked through the threshold it occurred to him that the scrapes taken from Guin could easily be there.

The concierge holo blinked into existence as they entered, flickering lightly as motes of dust floated through the projector. No human staff were out tonight it seemed, whether it was for privacy or money saving, Ryoma couldn't tell. "Networked suite for two?"

"Not tonight." Ryoma walked through it without stopping, the projection fragmenting on his body as he made a beeline for the pod room at the back. Inside was completely dark aside from the blue glow from each activated pod, the glass panel on the front of each corroded white coffin revealed the occupant and their vitals. The ceiling was unusually low, enough that Guin had to duck their head as they followed him, peering into each of the pods in turn. There were only twenty pods in total and only half in use so Ryoma quickly found him, quietly calling to Guin.

"That's him?" Guin looked through the glass at the man inside his face mostly obscured by the boxy visor, underwhelmed. "Can he really help us?"

"I don't know. But it's worth a shot." He clucked his tongue, and pressed the emergency stop button on the side of the pod. "Time to wake up, Mr. Rearden."

"The hell? My time isn't up already is it?" Dayne Rearden sat up as the door swung open. He lifted up his visor, eyes flung wide when he recognised Ryoma.

"It's you... from the showroom."

The colour drained from the scientist's face. He tried to stand, still wired in at the wrists, but fell back at the sight of Guin staring at him with the same intensity they'd looked at the tablet earlier. Ryoma wondered if it had been a good idea to bring them after all

"Yeah. It is. Sit."

Ryoma grabbed him by the shoulder and pushed him into the seat next to the pod, the wires that connected him to the sim tensing and snapping. The room around them was deathly quiet, other patrons configuring their pod either looked away or at least pretended not to notice.

There was a tense pause as he looked up at them both, eyes settling on Guin. Their towering presence. "I don't know you."

"No, you don't, but this might seem familiar..." Guin turned and lifted their hair up to show the scar on their neck. Ryoma watched as a mix of emotions swept through his face, settling on white faced terror, shaking his head weakly. "Y...you aren't supposed to remember. They said..."

"They said what?" Guin spat, their hand gripping so hard onto the pod door it began to creak and warp under the pressure. "Your corp friends tore my schematics from my skull, scraped out my brain, abused my body - and for what? For nothing. For junk you can't even sell."

"Are you here to kill me?"

"No, I want this to stop." Guin's voice shrunk to a forceful whisper, Ryoma caught their eye, willing that they could stay in control. "You're going to help us."

Careful darling, we still need him.

"I don't, I can't." He shook his head. "It's the company, they'll never stop, they've been trying for years, long before I was recruited. The technology just isn't there; they keep trying but none of it will work like, like you." He looked up at Guin with more than a hint of resentment.

"Better think twice before you say shit like that." Ryo scoffed. Maybe giving them a free swing wouldn't be so bad. A broken nose could be an improvement in some cases.

"Maybe they should have thought of that before annexing Hephaestus, and exiling us." The door to the VR pod creaked and crumpled under their hand, causing a new holo to flicker to life, warning them of an impending fine. It didn't matter, they wouldn't be coming back.

Ryoma waved it away sharply, leaning back against the adjacent pod. "Anything to say?"

"It started before my time, long before. If anyone asked we were told they were volunteers, it was a painless process but..."

"But you didn't believe that."

"I don't think anyone did," he glanced up at Guin. "We could see the damage done on entry, even on scans."

"So you just ignored it." Guin's face was impassive, and for a moment Ryoma wondered if they might actually do something rash. They had the strength for sure, but if they had the will was another case entirely.

Rearden looked away, Guin's presence alone enough to shame him. "This, this woman, she promised they'd buy us out once we cracked it. We'd be funded in full, we could do anything we wanted, see? Actually make something beneficial for once."

"And all it took was some kidnapped synths with their brains turned to soup, no skin off your nose," Ryoma said drily.

"I..." Dayne had run out of excuses, hunched and clammy he looked exhausted. "Please, I'll tell you everything, but not here, alone. There's a hotel down the street, the Palisade. My room is six one six, you can follow me up in a few minutes."

"If you try to run -"

"You'll find me, I understand." Without another word he stood brushed past them, still turned away from Guin.

"Do you think he'll run?" Guin asked, beginning to follow him, too soon for Ryo's taste.

"No, he knows it's over." Ryoma pushed the broken pod door closed. "Breathe, darling. We'll see this through."

Chapter Twenty Five

Neither of them spoke on the walk to the hotel, the noise of the night life filling the space between them. They walked confidently through the lobby, trying their best to fit in, gliding toward the elevators at the back. As the doors slid quietly shut, Guin leaned against the wall staring pensively into space, ignoring the stares of other occupants, tourists probably wondering where the nice part of the city was. After a few floors, they filtered out and the pair were left alone.

"You holding up ok? I've never seen you that angry before, or at all."

They were silent for a long time before releasing a strained, "no."

Of course they weren't, he knew that. "Not long now, darling."

The doors opened to an empty corridor and halfway down the door to room six one six, just slightly cracked open in an all too familiar scene. Something was wrong, this was too familiar, but Guin was already inside before he could stop them.

"Shit."

"No, no..." Guin's voice hitched in desperation. "We just spoke to him! Shit, what do we do?"

He grabbed their wrist before they could touch Rearden's body, limp on the cheap carpet. "Don't. Don't touch him."

Across the room a dry chuckle, alerted them to the fact they were not alone.

Ryoma had seen plenty of bodies before at this point in his life. Sometimes they were kids, runaways with shitty home lives, people who couldn't pay their debt left broken from repossession, the kind of fool who gambles big and disappears into the corporate machinery. And Serena. It never got easier.

But the killer wasn't usually present to mock him. He blinked a few times in succession. He still had Guin's lucky charm.

"Le Beau, baby, you kept me waiting again." The woman was perched on the stiff hotel bed, fingers tapping rhythmically on the gun. Her gaze fell to the body on the floor. "You just missed Mr. Rearden I'm afraid. Overseeing the abuse of synths like that is a scandal, it'll rock the industry. At least until the next news cycle. The shame must have been immense I'm sure." She shrugged nonchalantly, Rearden's blood pooling at her feet. The door was left tastefully intact, she hadn't replicated the mess she'd made of Ryo's house. Perhaps this was her idea of subtlety. "Too much, in fact. But this wraps it up don't you think? Case closed. Nothing more for the curious detective and his pet robot."

Guin winced visibly and tugged at Ryoma's wrist.

Don't.

"So that's it? Problem solved?" He took a cautious step back, they needed to get out of here. Guin could well be bulletproof but he certainly wasn't.

"That's all. The program was shut down, hit a few snags in production. When your friend put out their little search, your name was attached to it too. People will notice if you disappear now." She clucked her tongue, disappointed her fun had been ruined, very bad sport. At least he got what was what he needed.

"Now every connected synth knows, and everyone else will, soon enough. You'll be out of business."

"People will excuse a lot, especially when they live at our behest." Laux stepped distastefully over the viscera on the floor towards them. "And you do. Don't forget that, little doll."

Before Ryoma could stop them, Guin sprang at Odette, seizing her wrist and snapping her arm at the elbow. She yelled and shoved them back, the broken components piercing her pristine blue suit. The woman tried to hit back with her remaining arm but Guin was clearly stronger than she expected, shoving her to the ground. For the first time her expression was something other than smug.

She reached for the gun, but Ryoma snatched it up, feeling the weight of it in his steel hand.

"You think the people out there won't just turn you in if the price is right?" She stood, clutching her broken arm and looked at Ryoma. "You think the corp found your sister by chance the first time?"

"Fuck you." The gun felt disturbingly comfortable in his hand, an extension of his arm. It wouldn't take much to make her stop goading them. Barely any effort at all.

"Kill me and you'll be gutted in some alley somewhere. Just like her." She grinned through bloody teeth. "And they'll dissect that fucking thing like they should have in the first place."

A long moment later, he crushed the weapon in his fist, casting it down. She was right about that at least. They needed to disappear.

"We should go, Guin. Let's go." He took their wrist and pushed them back through the door. "She's done, it's done."

Odette shouted after them as they left, but Ryoma wasn't listening.

The floor was mercifully empty, the only other sign of life a swaying tourist trying to activate a key card reader repeatedly. The elevator to the exit was deathly silent. No exhalation, no sigh of relief from Guin. It's not like he could undo what had been done. His chest pounded so hard it was difficult to breathe but as the ground became closer he could feel the reality of their situation set in. "That was close, that was too close, darling."

"You really think I'd kill her?" Their eyes fixed to him. "That's why you wanted to leave isn't it?"

"I think you wanted to. And I think I'd let you."

"People like her can do whatever they want to people, and nothing comes of it." Their voice cracked and quavered, and he knew they'd be crying if they could. "What's the point of strength if I can't use it when I need to?"

"Cause we don't always need it," he pulled his lower eyelid down a little to show the extremely subtle reflection of the contact lens. The overlay in his peripheral vision told him the footage was being compressed and fed into the hive's memory shortly. "Your little gift came in handy."

"Ryo, you're..." They touched his cheek so gently he barely felt it, their despair softening.

"I told you, you're my lucky charm." He closed the gap between them. "It's a small start, Bio will have to lay low for a while, and be on their best behaviour. She'll be put out to pasture at least. It ain't much but," he gently elbowed their side. "Moves the dial a little in our favour huh?"

"It's something. Thank you. For taking me with you. For staying with me even when you saw...what you saw."

"Oh darling, what good would I be if I just up and left you?"

A smile tugged at the corner of their mouth, the same wry amusement they'd had that first night. "I suppose not."

The door pinged, and they were back to the start. He led the way out, past a bundle of luridly dressed guests who'd tried to shove their way into the compartment. Guin ducked through the doors. "Where do we go now?"

"Sylph had a little base set up in the Under, we can get all of this compressed and sent out. We can stop this."

"You really believe that?"

He remembered Serena's determination, her resolve in making things better for them and for everyone else. "I have to."

Chapter Twenty Six

"Aren't you meant to be working?" Guin looked up from their desk as the door clicked shut behind Ryoma. They were half dressed and surrounded by heaps of sketches, charcoal darkening the tips of their translucent lilac fingers and the morning suns pouring in through the window. A couple of weeks had passed since the Palisade and the news cycle was still going strong, a corp enforcer standing over a body could do that. Ryoma just hoped it would last, and lead to something long term.

"Your brother said you'd be here, thought I'd swing by." He sauntered over and placed the spare keycard on their desk, not wanting to be presumptuous. "I was being recognised a lot, a little embarrassing, dangerous too. Sylph's keeping a low profile too, so I figured I'd followed her lead."

"Can't be too careful."

"Although it did mean I found a med-mechanic pretty fast, though. I think she was happy to work on a celebrity, no matter how minor." He turned and showed them one of the clear dressings behind his ear.

"Looks good on you." They turned to face him, the shadow of their mechanical insides visible under their pale loose shirt. They'd decided to forgo all of their plating for now, their shoulders pulled back with confidence allowing light refracting through them. It suited them better. "So you couldn't stay away from me, huh?"

"Guess not." He smiled. "I don't know how much you've been following but BioMech is really panicking trying to run damage control. Dropping prices on upgrades, free patches and updates to pretty much everything they sell. They could have to hand back control of the colony to the governing council, not that they much want it. Never seen anything like it."

"That's, that's good, that's further than I thought it would spread. Maybe anyone that wants to hurt us will think twice. Do you think it will change anything?"

"If I'm honest? I don't know. Corps like BioMech, they're so embedded out here, it'll take a lot to shift them. But you never know, it might be the start of something."

"Could be. I just hope we've made it harder for them to do this again. Anyone with any hint of brain work will be on guard now." They tilted his chin back and smiled, leaving a grey smudge where they touched. "You look tired, Ryo."

"Been trying to keep pace with you for the past few weeks darling, stamina's not what it was. But I'd hate to miss anything." His eyes crinkled with his smile. "What about you darling? I know you don't need as much but..."

Their expression sank, and they shook their head turning back to finish blending the shadow of a Thresher breaching the sea's surface. "It's ok, you'll get there." He squeezed their shoulder, hoping that one day they could feel the peace he now felt, thanks to them. "Do you think you'll stay here, permanently?"

"Hephaestus meant a lot to me, but this is the closest I've felt in a long time. You're here, and my brother. That dip in the hive helped me remember a lot of things I love about being connected. I managed to get through to Autumn on Scylla too, Perci's become the star of the Satellite bar. Honorary staff member and everything. Not that there's any pests for her to catch." Guin's expression brightened. "What about you?"

"The upper-city might be a little hot for me for a while, maybe I'll stay down here too, if you don't mind me following you." Corp enforcers had still been crawling around his apartment building last time he'd checked. Time to start again, he supposed. It wasn't the first time. "I've been sleeping in the new office. Probably ain't the best for my back."

"My room is always open to you Ryo, although it's not much." Guin had said they needed more sunlight, now they had two. Their twin rays shining through their body, sending their reflections sparkling on the walls, filling the room.

"Lucky for me, 'not much' is perfect. If I'm fed and got a roof over my head, I ain't complaining."

"I'll take that as a yes." Guin smirked as his roundabout acceptance. "How is your new office?"

"Not sure I could call it an office yet. The co-op that owns the building said they'll let me stay for a while, if I work locally. And I think I can manage that, people are always tussling over any old thing."

"People are people anywhere I guess." They started, and began shuffling around the papers on their desk, until they found and produced a small business card, handing it to him with a grin. "I had this printed, just like yours."

River Sings!

Performing at The Serpent Lounge
Alternate Nights - Song Requests Considered

"I've found a new club in The Under, said I can sing anything I like, even if I have to stick with the pseudonym for now. I'll have them save a table for you, if you'll have it."

"Never had anyone sing for me before, sounds romantic." He turned the card over in his hands feeling the texture of the thick cardstock and embossed text under his fingertips. Even a business card from them was beautiful. Carefully, Ryoma perused through the messy stack of sketches on their desk, creatures winding around the paper in states of completion varying from loose pencil to smoothly inked painting. "Are these all your designs?"

"What do you think?" Guin hovered nervously.

"They're gorgeous," He stopped at a drawing half way down, a familiar little creature with a pair of tails. "Is this to go with your chest piece?" His arm circled their waist. He traced along its body, paying attention to the fine detailing of the scales. It was similar to his own, but drawn in their own liquid, inky style. "You like twin tails too huh?"

They smiled, trying to shuffle the rest of the drawings back on top. "That was... just a stupid idea, I was thinking of adding it somehow. That's rude of me."

"No, I like it." He uncovered the sketch for another look, "I really mean that much to you? You want me to be a part of you like that? Forever?"

They looked up at him, lips quivering trying to find the words amongst their feelings. They didn't need to; he could see how they felt. "Of course."

He looked back at the sketch. "So where will this one go? Show me."

"Sure...see? Then it wraps around the tail here, chasing the serpent." They pulled aside their shirt, tracing along the clear surface of their chest. "I thought it would make me more... complete."

They put their transparent hand on his steel one, gently pressed on the joints, working their way up his arm, testing it. "How's your arm? Still good I hope?"

"Never felt better. You've got a magic touch, angel."

"It's nothing. You just needed a little extra care, that's all." There was a lull, Guin's soft gaze warming him.

"You can stay tonight, if you like. If you're not busy."

"Nothing comes to mind, I think I could bear to stick around." He perched on the edge of the desk, even sat above them they barely had to look up.

"Good." Carefully, they ran their finger along his newly installed seam, the surrounding skin behind his ear was still tender. "Excited to try this little thing? Is it ready to go?"

"Yeah, the mech reckons so." He flushed at the sensitivity, the hunger behind their smile felt as a languid sensual melody. "Said it might take some getting used to, but I'm a quick study."

"I'd love to take you for a dive again, something simple on the hive, not work related. I think you'll be able to take it." Guin leaned over and drew a long line from his ear, down his throat, plucking at the buttons of his shirt.

"You know my limits."

Epilogue

"Beautiful set." Ryoma grinned as Guin joined him in his regular booth at the Serpent, their bright crystal body glistened beneath their dress, the low back revealing their newest modification. The puncture cracking along their back had been sealed but rather than match the grey-lilac crystal, they'd chosen to fill the space with shining veins of silver, drawing the eye to the star reaching between their shoulders. "As always."

"I thought you'd like the new songs." They sat next to him, legs thrown over his lap, they kicked their feet. "I haven't written in years and now I can hardly stop. Funny isn't it? You bring it out in me." They craned their neck around to catch the eye of a waiter but it was so busy tonight, they were lost in the fray. "Do you want anything from the bar?"

"You know what I like." He mouthed at their throat, using the high slit on their dress to find his way in. In the past year their collection of engravings had grown substantially, leaving their body beautifully textured all over. He wished he could feel every part of them there and then, no matter that the bar was packed.

"I don't think that's on the menu." They smiled, voice husky and low against his ear, but they didn't stop him.

"Shame, I'll have to wait." He pouted in feigned offence, his hand settling high up their thigh as Guin hailed a passing waiter with a tray to apologetically order theirs and Ryo's usual. "You've settled in well around here, you're quite popular with the locals."

They glanced around at the crowded bar, tucking their hair tuck. "I'm barely an opening act without a band but I have had a few compliments. A little birdie said you've been busy, detective. You got a new case?"

"A couple actually." He actually had a backlog for the first time ever, he'd probably have to hire a secretary at least to keep his eclectic filing in order. He squeezed their knee. "At least one of them said I was highly recommended. You wouldn't have something to do with that, would you?"

"It was nothing really, I let a few people know there was a new PI in the Under, mostly organic but trustworthy. Charming too."

"Hmm, I'm sure that's what sold it." They paused as their drinks were placed in front of them, the contents refracting on the table, light through an aquarium. "If you're interested, I've got a synth's body gone AWOL whilst they were submerged. Some well to-do type with a luxury build moonlighting down here. Brain left completely untouched, didn't even notice the disconnect until they tried to exit. Wants it dealt with quietly, since they weren't meant to be here at all."

"Sounds like vultures, very good ones."

"That's what I reckoned, too clean to be untargeted." Under his fingers he could feel the textures engraved into their surface, like a needle on a record he wanted to make them sing again. "I was hoping you'd want to help, as a consultant. Figured they might see you as a friendly face and remember something. You are my lucky charm, after all." He knew their answer already, he didn't need a seam for that.

"Of course, but," they looked at him, metering their words carefully. "But ...maybe tomorrow morning? I had a little something planned for you this evening. A thank you, if you will. A gift, for your birthday."

"Oh? I thought the new songs were for me. Unless you got another Ryo I don't know about. Can I have a hint?"

"So impatient aren't you Ryo? You'll have to see." They drained their glass and stood, their unhitched dress flowing back into place. "Let's go, they won't hold our room for long."

Intrigued, he followed them into the night, through the now familiar maze of the under-city. All right angles and shadow, he let his siren lead him astray, mind awash with possibilities. It had showered earlier that night, sharpening the edges of every footstep until Guin stopped suddenly in front of a building with a flickering sign for a restaurant. They depressed the intercom button and spoke.

"I have a reservation under River?"

"Dinner?"

It looked deserted from the outside, but that wasn't always an indicator the place was abandoned. Looking derelict was good camouflage.

"Not quite, though you'll be hungry afterwards." The door clicked and slid open so quietly it could have been a breath.

The private pool was already prepared for them, sunk deep into the floor and covering almost the whole room. The only light sources inside were the soft blues of the gel and a small screen on the wall that read 'simulation compiled and ready.'

Carefully, Guin slipped off their shimmering shoes by the pool, the light rippling from their surface onto the ceiling. They climbed straight in, the fabric of their dress flowed freely, blooming around them.

"You know how I said the hive remembers everyone it touches? Well I- I found something she'd been working on."

He stared into the pool, the weight of memory behind him, the bloodied ghost he'd seen a year ago. "She'd loved to dive, always wanted me to join her."

"I spent a long time digging, piecing it together and Sylph helped to fill some gaps too." It's only a snapshot, but you seemed so heartbroken when you lost all your pictures of her, and all for my sake." They reached out to invite him in, their glassy body almost a lilac shadow. "Would you like to see?"

He took their hand and lowered himself in, prepared this time for his surroundings to start to shift, anticipation rising in his chest as a landscape began to form in his mind's eye. Distantly he heard sounds like rain on a corrugated roof. Exactly like it, in fact. He was about to speak, when his mind connected to theirs directly, streams leading into the ocean, and everything came into focus.

About the Author

Franklyn (They/She) has been writing on and off since their teens, largely inspired by the sci-fi & horror movies that wormed into their brain when they left the tv on at night. They enjoy writing about transhumanism, the struggle for bodily autonomy and finding love. They're based in the south of England and run a two person book club with their partner, reading brick sized sci-fi novels and comparing notes.

Milton Keynes UK
Ingram Content Group UK Ltd.
UKHW022223050424
440549UK00004B/178

9 798224 827572